A
Choice to
Cherish

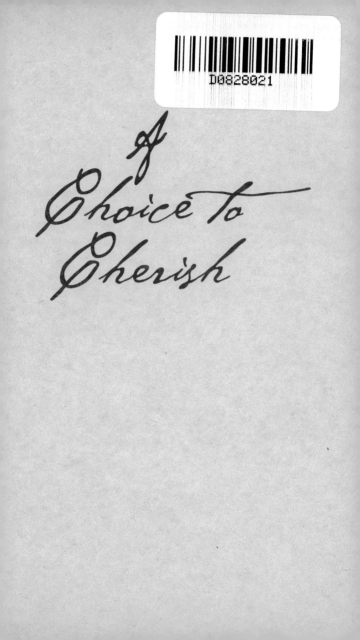

A Novel

A Choice to Cherish

ALAN MAKI

Steeple
Hill®

Published by Steeple Hill Books™

STEEPLE HILL BOOKS

Steeple
Hill®

Recycling programs
for this product may
not exist in your area.

ISBN-13: 978-0-373-78656-5
ISBN-10:   0-373-78656-5

A CHOICE TO CHERISH

Steeple Hill Books/October 2008

First published by Broadman & Holman Publishers in 2000

www.SteepleHill.com

Printed in U.S.A.

To my wife, Sharon,
and our children,
Shaylan, Shaun, and Mark

Acknowledgments

I wish to thank Nell and Dr. Theophilus Erskine Ross III for their medical expertise regarding this story. Thanks to George Dunlap for his wonderful gift to store my every written word. LaRoy Williamson came through with countless hours of work preparing the manuscript, for which I am grateful. Mike Pagliara also contributed his time and computer skills, and I am blessed by his friendship. Ken Shetler enriched my novel by sharing a personal experience which I weaved into the heart and soul of the book. Hugs and kisses to my wife Sharon and son Shaun for their typing and critiquing, and to my daughter Shaylan, my son Mark, and my parents for their enthusiastic support of my writing and my dreams. To Vicki Crumpton and Kim Overcash at B&H, who embraced this story with joy and encouraging words, I give thanks. Also, heartfelt thanks to Doug Nichols of Action International Ministries for deeply impacting my life and church. Above all, praise God for his divine guidance through the promptings of the Holy Spirit during work on this touching book.

Chapter One

Grandpa's House

When my father called to tell me about Grandpa's impending death, I must admit I wasn't concerned. I hadn't seen much of Grandpa in my almost twenty years of life, and the brief family visits we had shared had been wrought with a curious tension between my grandfather and my dad. More than ten years had passed since I last tossed a baseball with Grandpa, and all I really remembered was trying to catch a fastball that was too fast for a nine-year-old. The ball skipped off the top of my misplaced glove and hit me squarely on the nose. The blood I licked with my tongue ended up being thicker than that between relations, and my family left Grandpa's house that day for good. I came to believe that that hardball had caused feelings too hard for reconciliation.

"Alan, your grandfather's dying, and I want you to stay with him for a while," my father told me on the phone, grabbing my full attention. "You're through with your exams today, right?"

I would take my last exam in one hour; then I was free for the Christmas break. "Yeah, but I was planning a ski trip this weekend," I protested, "and it's my birthday the twenty-fourth. Besides, I don't even know Grandpa. What's his problem anyway?"

"He had a heart attack a few months ago, then another two weeks ago. I didn't know about the second one until a doctor called last night to tell me his heart's giving out. He's got a thickening of the heart muscle and lots of damage. It's called cardiomyopathy."

I absorbed the news, then blurted, "Where is he?"

"He's home."

"His home? In Montana somewhere?"

"Yeah, in Darby. He wants to die at home, but I'm told he needs someone there." After a short pause, Dad added, "Look, I can't get off work until Christmas. If I get you a plane ticket, will you stay with him for a week or so?"

Reluctantly, I flew from Detroit to Missoula, Montana, the next morning. In my mind, both my holiday vacation and my twentieth birthday were ruined. Taking care of a bedridden old man whom I hardly knew was not my idea of a Christmas season—or a birthday.

The flight itself was uneventful until the plane descended out of the clouds and I saw the mountains below. Grandpa had made the move from Michigan to Montana a few years ago, but I had never been west to see him. My first look at the snow-covered Rockies elated me.

Once on the ground at Missoula International Airport, I rescued my two suitcases from the baggage area and followed the signs to Hertz Rent A Car. It "hurt," all right, filling up my credit card, but the new indigo blue Taurus awaiting my arrival fit me well.

Following the directions my father had given me, I drove two-lane Highway 93 all the way to Darby, population 625, some 62 miles south of Missoula in the Bitterroot Valley.

The hour-and-a-quarter drive was the prettiest I'd ever made. Snowcapped, jagged, forested mountains, one after another, greeted me on my right while smaller, more rounded and brown mountains closed in on my left as I traveled down the valley floor. The sky was a rich blue with nary a cloud and seemed bigger somehow than back home. Small western towns popped up every ten or fifteen miles on Highway 93, with names like Lolo, Florence, Stevensville, Victor, and Hamilton.

Because my father's directions only got me to Darby, I stopped at a convenience store called Mr. T's to inquire about my grandfather's whereabouts. I parked beside a red sports car bearing a license plate that read "PSALM 1."

The pretty but flighty cashier inside "T's" was just a high school kid who seemed too self-involved to know about an unrelated, dying old man. I borrowed her phone book, but there was no listing for my grandfather.

A young, red-headed woman, perhaps twenty years old, caught my attention as she approached the checkout counter. She was beautiful in her blue denim skirt and jacket, and her big, blue eyes were gazing right at me.

"Excuse me," she said, smiling. "Did I hear you say George Maki's your grandfather?"

Feeling a bit uncomfortable, I shifted my weight and uttered, "Yeah."

She extended her right hand toward me. "I'm Robin Patterson, a friend of your grandfather's."

I grinned and shook her hand. "Ah, I'm Alan Maki. Nice to meet me…uh…you," I stumbled, blushing.

Robin kept smiling. Her perfect teeth were the whitest I'd ever seen. I imagined that my face was the reddest she'd ever laid eyes on.

"Listen," she said, "go four miles south of town and turn right just before the bridge over the Bitterroot River. That's the West Fork. Drive half a mile, and George's place is the little white house on the right. Look for the white fence. You can't miss it."

I walked outside with her and thanked her for her help. She climbed into the car with the godly license plate, and even I could discern that Robin was a heavenly girl. Someone "up there" had broken the mold with her.

Smitten, I wondered if I'd ever see her again.

Several minutes later, I discovered that Robin Patterson's directions were accurate. Just beyond a mailbox with "Maki" painted on it, I turned onto the ninety-foot paved driveway to the house. My eyes darted from the little house to a small red barn to the south, then to the barking German shepherd running toward my car. As I stopped alongside an old, black Chevy truck in front of a one-car garage, the dog stood on its hind legs and pawed vigorously at my driver's-side window.

"Get down!" I cried, rolling down the window. The dog kept at it. Realizing the rental car's paint job was in jeopardy, I flung open the door.

"Get away!" I gasped, anticipating the teeth. Instead, I received the slap of a long, wet tongue on the back of my left hand.

"Buck!" A high-pitched voice rang out from the

house. A short, elderly woman leaned out the front door. Buck loped toward her.

"Hello!" I hailed. "Is this where George Maki lives?"

The woman waited until I reached the porch before answering, "Yes. Are you Alan?"

I nodded. She grabbed the dog's collar with one hand and held the storm door open for me with the other.

"The dog's still young," she explained. "Come in out of the cold!"

It was warm inside the house, but dark.

"Please have a seat," invited the woman, "and I'll see if your grandfather is awake." She headed toward a back room, with Buck trotting after her. Over her shoulder she said, "My name's Opal, by the way. I'm a hospice nurse."

I took off my leather jacket, tossed it on an armchair beneath the only window in the living room, and sat down in another chair. Short chintz draperies filtered the light of the midafternoon sun. On the rug-covered floor in the center of the room sat an antique coffee table. Hanging on the blue-gray barn-wood wall behind a wood-burning stove was an old wooden sign that read, "Notis you: Who's to givit you promisson for huntit my land? Better you to lookit outdt else I sootit you wit da 2-pipe sotgun." I couldn't help but smile.

"He's still asleep." Opal was back, carrying her purse and coat. Buck was with her.

"Listen," she said, "I've been here quite a while waiting for you, and I've got to go. I'll leave a list of medications and a time schedule." She took a piece of paper out of her purse and handed it to me as I stood up from the chair.

"Leaving so soon?" I asked, suddenly apprehensive. I

glanced at the list, and the responsibility distressed me. "Can I do this?"

Opal grinned. "You can do it," she assured me, moving to the front door. "There's plenty of food in the kitchen, and the dog food is in the pantry. Wood's stacked out back."

With the door opened, she added, "The medicines are on the dresser in George's bedroom. I'll be back Monday afternoon to check on things." Then she was gone. The door clicking shut made my stomach sink.

I folded the paper and shoved it into my back pants pocket. Buck emitted a short whine, reminding me of his support. I reached a hand toward the dog.

"We might as well be pals," I said, hearing the Chevy truck's engine start up. I stopped stroking the dog and walked through the dining area past an oak table and four chairs. A small kitchen was located to the right, but I veered left and entered a short hallway. On the left was an open door, so I stepped inside, finding a large bathroom decorated in shades of blue.

As I left the room, Buck trotted to the closed door at the end of the hallway. Sure that Grandpa was on the other side, I moved toward the door, only to pull up short at an array of family pictures displayed on the right side wall.

A large photo of Grandpa and Grandma Joyce, taken perhaps a year or two before her death in 1978, was the centerpiece, surrounded by about twenty smaller pictures. I quickly found two oldies of me with my younger sister, Linda, and my parents, along with my high school graduation picture. There were a couple pictures of my father as a young man and another of a man I thought was my grandfather's brother, Leonard. A half-dozen others depicted my grandmother in attractive poses, while some more recent photographs showed Grandpa in camouflage hunting clothes. An old, yellowed, black-and-white photograph of a young man and woman in wedding attire hung above all the rest.

Buck's scratching at the closed door drew me away from the pictures. I quietly turned the doorknob. Buck would have none of it and bulled his way into the room. As the door swung wide, I laid eyes on the old man in his bed. His head was sticking out from under his blanket and was elevated by a pillow. He didn't move as the dog paced from one side of the bed to the other.

Gingerly, I approached, struggling to recognize the grandfather I had not seen in ten-and-a-half years. His face looked old and gaunt, and the wavy, wheat-colored hair of his younger days was gone, leaving a bald head. His nose was narrow, widening at the bottom where a nasal cannula was inserted into his nostrils. His lips were pencil-thin, and his chin was quite pointed.

Suddenly the blue eyes in the face popped open, startling me. They then squeezed shut as though what they had seen was too horrendous to look at. I stepped back, tripping over Buck, and almost fell down. Buck, bewildered, dashed out of the room. I expected the commotion to wake up Grandpa, but he remained still. I watched him for a minute, noting the shallowness of his breathing. Then my eyes began to wander.

To the right of the bed, placed below a shaded window and next to a portable oxygen tank, sat an old dresser with four plastic medicine bottles lined up in a perfect row on top, surely courtesy of Nurse Opal. I then looked farther right at a three-tier, hardwood bookshelf filled with more than a hundred books. Above the books, a wooden, square-faced clock was bracketed on the wall, and next to it hung a colorfully dyed wool rug, about four feet long and three feet wide.

At the right foot of the bed sat a metal folding chair with a padded seat. To the left of the bed was a teak end table with a simple glass-based lamp sitting on it, along with a small picture of my grandmother, a Bible, and a pair of reading glasses. Behind me to my left stood a five-foot-tall, black steel, square-bodied floor safe. I peered at the combination lock in the large, sealed door. Naturally, my curiosity peaked. I wondered what was hidden inside.

Glancing at Grandpa, I noticed a framed print of Jesus hanging on the wall above the head of the bed. Only the head and shoulders had been painted, and they were life-size. The dark brown, glistening eyes seemed to look through me.

"I've heard your grandpa's got religion now, so don't be surprised if he hits you over the head with it," my father had warned me earlier in the day at the Detroit Metropolitan Airport. This Jesus picture certainly hinted at religion, as did the Bible on the table; but by the looks of Grandpa, I doubted he was strong enough to hit me with anything.

Chapter Two

Grandpa

Buck reentered the room and began pacing again. I decided to sit in the chair and wait for Grandpa to awaken, but the moment the chair creaked, he coughed and bolted upright.

"What's going on? Who are you?"

I stood up and grinned. "I'm Alan, your grandson," I said, looking for a glimmer of recognition on the old man's face. "Dale's son," I added after a moment.

Grandpa, dressed in a red-plaid pajama top, stared hard at me. He removed the nasal cannula, which included a long tube connected to the oxygen tank, and said with surprising warmth, "Come closer, my boy, so I can see how you grew up." I moved my six-foot, medium frame around the right side of the bed.

"Let me touch you," he said quietly.

Raising my hand toward his, I saw a tear slip from his right eye and into the hollow of his cheek. Then our hands clasped. His was cold.

"You've got a strong grip, son," he told me, squeezing tighter. "I was praying for your trip. You're an answer to prayer." With those words, he let loose and I pulled my hand back, wondering what an answer-to-prayer was supposed to say.

Buck suddenly jumped up beside me and rested his front paws on the bed, whimpering like a love-starved puppy.

"Buck!" Grandpa exclaimed. The dog licked his master's fingers as his long tail wagged against my leg.

"Go lie down, Buck," Grandpa finally said, tiring out and slumping back onto his pillow. The dog dropped to the floor and began wandering about the room.

"Alan, bring that folding chair here next to me and sit down." Following directions better than Buck, I did as I was told. Grandpa wanted to talk, but would we relate to one another? I wondered.

"The last time I laid eyes on you, you were nine years old. Now you're just a week and a day from twenty."

I nodded my head, impressed that a grandpa who had been so removed from my life would know such a thing. "On December 24," I stated.

"Well, son, I'm glad you're here. It's been a long time." He closed his eyes as if envisioning the spent past. "What a waste, all those years."

I squirmed and changed the subject. "How old is Buck?"

"Ah, Buck," he said, looking at me and grinning. "He's young like you. Just a year and a half. Doesn't know I'm dying. An older dog would probably sense it, but not Buck. Too young to know much."

I sensed that Grandpa, who I knew had taught high school English, thought that I was also too green to possess much knowledge, so I chose to cite my accomplishments. "I noticed my high school graduation picture hanging in the hallway," I remarked, prefacing my subject.

"Yes, your mother sent it to me—unbeknownst to your dad, I figure."

"Did you know I was the salutatorian of my class?" I asked, speaking the line I couldn't wait to get off my tongue.

"Who was the valedictorian?" Grandpa shot back, perhaps innocently, but the insinuation stung me.

After a short hesitation, I rebounded. "Bruce Berryman was, but both of us received academic scholarships to the University of Michigan." The words came forth a little loudly, but I made sure Grandpa heard them.

He simply nodded his bony head, a reaction with which I was disappointed until he said, "I'm proud of you, Alan. Michigan is a fine school." He pulled his blanket up to his chin. "Did you play baseball in high school?"

The question astonished me. Baseball had been my whole world in high school. I had starred in Babe Ruth, American Legion, and varsity ball, and it seemed like every Tom, Dick, and Harry followed my career—yet my own grandfather knew nothing of it. What on earth had happened between my parents and me and my grandpa? Was it all because of that bloody nose when I was nine?

"I lettered three years on varsity," I stated proudly. "Pitched two no-hitters and won twenty games for Belleville High School."

Grandpa was tickled by this news. "You don't say! How fast can you throw it?"

I grinned. "Eighty-five, eighty-six."

Grandpa raised his eyebrows. "That's hummin' it." He coughed, sucked in some air, and asked, "Are you playing for Michigan?"

"Freshman ball last spring. I won three, lost two. Gotta get better." Grandpa didn't respond, so I added, "Been lifting weights to get stronger."

Grandpa reached for the nasal cannula lying on the bed beside him. "You're getting stronger; I'm getting weaker," he mumbled, shakily poking the tubing up his nose. After drawing some oxygen, he asked what time it was. I gazed at my wristwatch. It showed 5:31, but I realized that was Eastern time.

"It's 3:30," I answered, looking at the clock on the wall. My eyes rested on the wool rug hanging oddly by the clock.

"Um, why is that rug on the wall?"

Grandpa muttered, "I thought it was around noon; no wonder I'm so hungry." His voice trailed off. Then he smiled.

"That rug is a special rug." Deep crow's-feet wrinkles tugged at the corners of his eyes. "It's a Finnish *ryijy* rug made by your great-grandmother Marja about sixty years ago. She stained it with homemade vegetable dyes."

"It's a wedding *ryijy,*" he continued. "Your grandmother and I stood on it when we were married. Finnish tradition. Oh, and the pinewood clock: that clock traveled in a wooden crate from Finland in my father's care, wrapped in this lamb's-wool blanket." Grandpa held up the edge of his blanket and jiggled it. "Kinda thin and scratchy now," he snickered.

I shook my head. "Amazing."

"Son, there are lots of amazing things to discover in this house. How long are you staying?"

"I fly home a week from tomorrow, on the twenty-fourth," I informed him. "That's—"

"Your birthday!" Grandpa blurted.

"That's not what I was going to say," I chuckled. "I was going to say, 'That's probably the day my dad flies out here.'"

Grandpa's smile faded.

I considered pressing him about his reaction, but he rolled onto his side, away from me. *Later,* I decided.

Buck's wet nose touched my hand. I patted the dog's head, then asked Grandpa, "So, you're hungry?"

"Yes," came the soft reply.

"What can you eat?"

"I can chew anything you can. I've done quite well in the teeth department for a sixty-four-year-old man." He turned toward me and made a big, open-mouth smile.

I sat in a mild state of shock, not because of Grandpa's teeth but because of his age. I had figured he was well into his seventies, and in his weakened condition he looked it. But he was young. Too young to be dying.

"You're sixty-four?" I uttered stupidly.

"How old did you think I was, Alan?"

Thinking fast, I said, "Oh, about sixty-five or sixty-six, I guess."

He grinned. "You're lying, right?"

He had me, and my look showed it.

The old man waved a hand in front of his face as if brushing away a fly. "Don't worry about it," he said, letting me off the hook. "This old body is just an earth suit. I got the most out of it I could, and it's just about time to acquire a better model."

I wondered what he meant, but he chose not to elaborate. Instead, he asked me to heat up the leftover lasagna in the refrigerator.

"But first," he said, "take Buck and go look around the place while there's still daylight. I've got five acres with a nice bunch of blue spruce trees beyond the barn."

I scooted my chair back and stood up. Buck moved with me away from the bed.

"Did you find your bedroom yet?"

I shook my head.

"It's off the northwest corner of the living room. Small, but a place to lay your head."

"That's fine," I assured Grandpa. Moving toward the door, I said, "I'll grab my bags from the car, and I'll be back soon with the lasagna. Come on, Buck!"

I heard Grandpa cough, then call after me, "Your bathroom's there too."

Buck ran ahead of me to the living room, where I grabbed my jacket.

"Let's go, Buck," I said, opening the front door. Buck darted out, and I followed.

After collecting my bags from the car, I left Buck outside and located my tiny bedroom. A twin bed, a lop-sided dresser, and a portable, six-hanger valet stand were crammed between the lilac-colored walls. I dropped my bags on the mattress beneath a poster depicting an aerial view of two sparkling lakes surrounded by green forest, then opened a creaky door at the left side of the bed. I looked into an ugly, fire-pink-colored bathroom where someone (obviously not an interior decorator) had squeezed a toilet, a sink, and a shower stall.

"Yikes," I said, grimacing. I shut the door and plopped myself onto the bed beside my luggage. As my back sank into the mushy mattress, the box springs squeaked and clacked. I gazed up at the paint-peeled ceiling, also noting the light fixture that held six dead flies.

"Home, sweet home," I muttered.

Chapter Three

The Tree

Since the valley floor was free of snow and I was wearing sneakers, I chose to tour Grandpa's acreage on the run. With Buck trotting beside me, I jogged south along the white wooden fence that fronted West Fork Road.

After a hundred yards the white fence intersected an unpainted wooden fence that separated Grandpa's property from his neighbor's. I followed the second fence westward to a wooded area at the base of a steep hill. Not wanting to run up the incline, I turned north toward the blue spruce trees Grandpa had mentioned.

Suddenly a deer appeared to my left, bounding through the woods and up the hill. I stopped to get a good look, and my heart leaped when I saw it was a large whitetail buck. Buck got excited, too, and kept barking until I began running again. Then he ran with me.

I admired the spruce trees, which numbered about

twenty, as we went past. One in particular, I thought, would make a fine Christmas tree.

At the small barn behind the house, we stopped running. I stepped inside the barn. Buck followed for a moment, then changed his mind and ran toward the house.

There was little to be found in the barn. An ancient tractor looked as if it hadn't been used for quite awhile. A long workbench was speckled with various tools and mice droppings. On one end of the workbench some boxes were piled. One was marked "Christmas," another "Books," a third "Clothes," and two others were unmarked. The clothes box's corners had been chewed by rodents.

Shrugging, I left the barn and walked to the house, where Buck was lapping water out of a bowl beside the porch. A bunch of cut wood was neatly stacked there alongside a small pine box overflowing with kindling.

I grabbed two pieces of firewood and entered the house through the back door, keeping Buck out. At the living room stove, I gently pitched the wood into the dying fire.

Leaving my jacket on a chair, I walked into the kitchen, which contained an electric oven and a refrigerator. A black rotary phone hung on the wall next to the fridge. Above the sink was a window overlooking the western side of the property and the barn to the southwest. Wood cabinets encased the window. I opened the cupboards nearest the sink and found them filled with old dishes, pots and pans, a toaster, dish soap, and a rack of stainless steel silverware.

"No microwave," I moaned as I wondered how I could possibly manage without one. Yet within twenty minutes I was carrying two plates loaded with piping hot lasagna, toasted garlic bread, and applesauce into Grandpa's bedroom. He sat up as I switched on the ceiling light and approached his bed.

"Dinner is served," I said with a grin.

Grandpa laughed as he reached down beside the bed for a tray. "You were banging around so much that I thought a drummers' convention had convened in my kitchen!" He settled the tray on his lap, and I slipped his plate onto the tray.

"Here you go," I said, giving Grandpa a fork, "but be careful; the lasagna's hot. Besides that, you might bite into a drumstick from the convention."

He laughed, and it was a laugh I liked. I smiled at him, suddenly wishing I could've known him better.

"We've got to pray first," my grandfather said, eyeing me closely. "How 'bout it?"

I stared at Grandpa, holding my plate and realizing he was waiting for me to do the honors. I got a sick feeling inside.

"You're asking me to pray?"

"Sure," he said, nodding.

"I don't really...know how," I mumbled.

A slight grin creased his face. "Are you telling me you've never prayed before?" he asked without a hint of provocation.

I gave the question some consideration. Had I ever prayed?

"Not really," I said, perplexed.

Grandpa kept smiling at me. "What about when you're out on the mound and the opposing team has bases loaded, nobody out, and the meat of their batting order coming up? Have you ever been in that jam?"

Grinning, I admitted, "Yeah, this past spring. Bases

loaded, nobody out, but the seventh man in the lineup came to the plate."

Grandpa's eyes lit up. "Well," he prodded, "what went through your mind when you faced that guy?" He wriggled his eyebrows in anticipation.

I laughed. "You mean, did I pray?"

Grandpa beamed. He had nailed me, and he knew it.

Shaking my head, I confessed, "I remember saying, 'Help me, God.'"

"That's a prayer!" my grandfather declared, clapping his hands. "So let's do it again before our food freezes up!" Giving in, I lowered my head. I was uncomfortable, but I did remember hearing someone pray over Thanksgiving dinner a few times.

After wetting my lips with my tongue, I said quietly, "God, thanks for this meal." I took a deep breath, then added, "And thanks for my grandpa."

So far so good, I thought, but then I was at a loss. I looked to the old man for help. His head was bowed and his hands were clasped. He didn't move a muscle, so I rallied to help myself.

"Amen!" I said, ending the short prayer.

Grandpa looked up and smiled. "Nice blessing," he responded before digging into the lasagna.

Relieved, I sat in the chair and balanced my plate on my lap.

"So, then," Grandpa said between bites, "what happened in that ball game?"

I gave him a look. "You mean with that seventh batter? He hit into a double play, and only one run scored." Cockily, I added, "I struck the next guy out, and we won the game by a run."

Grandpa eased back into his pillow and remarked, "I really wish I'd been there." The sorrow in his voice touched my heart. I hardly knew this man, yet there was something special about him. Maybe it was just the fact that he was my grandfather. Perhaps it was his smarts and wiliness, or his unmistakable desire to have been an integral part of my life. Or maybe, simply…love.

We ate quietly for a few minutes; then I blurted, "Grandpa, ah…can I call you Grandpa?"

He chuckled. "Well, it seems more appropriate than Grandma, doesn't it?"

Grinning, I replied, "OK, Grandpa, you didn't tell me the prettiest woman in Montana was your buddy."

"Robin!" he exclaimed, his eyes dancing. "She attends Community Church with me. A great girl!"

"What's she doing in a tiny place like Darby?" I wondered aloud.

"Well, she graduated from Darby High School, then she attended college in Oregon for two years. Now she's back here working to make some money so she can finish her education."

"Hmmm," I hummed, doing a quick calculation. "She must've graduated from high school in 1993, a year ahead of me."

"That's correct. She was the valedictorian." Grandpa gave me a playful look. Before I could react, he added matter-of-factly, "Of course, there were only forty-one students in her class."

"There were 450 in my class at Belleville High School," I stated proudly.

Grandpa grinned. "Robin's a great girl," he repeated. "She and her family were my closest neighbors when I first moved here, so I used to see her all the time. She mowed my lawn for me one summer, most of the time for free. Then she moved north of town. Anyway, I still see her at church, and she drops by now and then. We've developed a good friendship."

Finished with our meal, I took Grandpa's tray and set my plate on his. "You know what we need?" I said. "A Christmas tree, right over there." I pointed to a spot beside the steel floor safe.

My grandfather raised his eyebrows. "Did you see any good ones out there in my blue spruce patch?"

"Yeah, I saw one." I stood up. "I'll go and get it right now. There's just enough daylight."

"There's a tree stand and some decorations in the barn," Grandpa said as I started out of the bedroom.

"OK," I replied, already knowing where to find the box.

"There's a saw there too!" he called after me. I grabbed my jacket from the chair in the living room and hustled out the back door, meeting Buck at the bottom of the porch. The dog followed me to the barn, then across the field to the evergreen tree of my choice.

It took less than a minute to work the saw blade through the tree's trunk. I dragged the tree to the back porch, then returned the saw to the barn. I retrieved the Christmas box and carried it and the tree into Grandpa's bedroom, where I planted the tree in the stand next to the big safe.

"Before you start decorating, Alan, please take me to the bathroom," Grandpa requested. He removed the nasal cannula, muttering, "I'm tired of this thing." Swinging his legs off the bed, he leaned over and shut off the valve on the oxygen tank. I helped him to his feet.

"Onward," he directed, and we started toward the

blue-colored bathroom. As we walked, I noted that my grandfather was only about an inch shorter than me, and in spite of his sickness, his posture was erect. He was well-built for a man his age.

"I can handle this part by myself," Grandpa declared at the bathroom. His breathing was labored now. "Go ahead and start decorating. I'll call you when I'm finished."

Back in the bedroom, I quickly dug four strings of red, green, and blue lights out of Grandpa's Christmas box and wound them around the tree. Then I speedily hung three dozen ornaments and ten plastic candy canes on the limbs.

When I heard the bathroom door open, I hurried to meet Grandpa. His breathing was still irregular, but that became the last thing on his mind after he'd laid eyes on the Christmas tree.

"You're done already!" he exclaimed, giving me a serious look. "I wanted to hang a few things on the tree myself!" He shook free from my hand, stumbled once, then gazed into the Christmas box. He happily announced, "The star's still here!"

"Yeah," I said, "and a carving of an angel, and a little blue-and-white flag."

Grandpa reached into the box and withdrew the small flag on a stick. "This is a Finnish flag," he told me. I nodded knowingly.

"December 6 was the seventy-eighth anniversary of Finnish independence," Grandpa continued. He poked the flag's stick into a branch of the tree and was careful to make sure it stayed put.

"Now, then," he said, reaching into the box again, "this angel was carved by my father when I was a baby." Grandpa straightened up and held the wooden artifact for me to see. Its appearance personified a boy angel, painted white and gold, with tiny wings. "My mother said I looked like an angel when I was born, so Poppa made this."

I eyed the carving. "You mean that's supposed to be you?"

Grandpa chuckled. "Yes. In my younger days I was rather cute." The angel was fashioned with a small wire hook glued to the back, and Grandpa hung it in the middle of the tree.

Returning to the box, he pulled out the final object, a gold-sequined star.

"Would you bring that chair over here, Alan?"

I knew what he was thinking about doing, so I tried to circumvent him. "That's OK, Grandpa. I can reach the top."

Grandpa grinned at me. "Yes, but I can't. The chair, please."

"You sure?"

Grandpa impatiently jabbed the air with his hand. "I'm getting older by the minute, son," he said sarcastically. "I've always put the star on top of the Christmas tree."

I set the chair close to the tree, and taking Grandpa's left arm, I upthrust his body as he climbed onto the chair. He shuddered for a moment, and I grabbed onto him with both hands. He reached up and placed the star on the highest sprig.

"Got it!" Grandpa proclaimed. Then I helped him down and into bed. Coughing now, he found the cannula and wasted no time slipping it on. He turned on the oxygen and breathed deeply for a short spell, never taking his eyes off the star on top of the tree.

I picked up the chair and carried it back to the side of

the bed. Sitting in it, I sighed with relief, thankful that Grandpa hadn't broken his neck. How would I have explained that one to Nurse Opal? I wondered, dreading the thought.

"You know," Grandpa said between breaths, "we're still missing something."

I gazed at the ornaments on the tree and concluded that everything seemed complete to me. "What do you mean?" I questioned.

Grandpa smiled. "It's not what's missing *on* the tree," he said softly, "but what's missing *under* the tree."

"No presents," I uttered.

"That's right," said Grandpa, his eyes twinkling, "no gifts. But we can fix that right away."

I stared at him with a dumb look on my face. "How?" Grandpa grinned like a child holding a wonderful secret.

Chapter Four

The Safe

"What have you got in mind, Grandpa?" I urged, anxious to share in his glee.

Chuckling softly, he said, "38-12-33." Then he gave me an expectant look.

Since the numbers he had rattled off meant nothing to me, I responded flippantly, "Sounds like a lady with an extremely tight belt." Grandpa laughed louder and pointed toward the Christmas tree.

I studied the shape of the tree from top to bottom, then announced, "It looks like 12-38-83 to me!" This time Grandpa clutched his stomach and belly-laughed. His reaction made me laugh too.

"Not the tree!" he exclaimed.

I looked again to the corner of the room in question and focused on the big floor safe and its combination lock.

"The safe!" I cried. "You're trusting me with the combination?" I shook my head, reminding him that he barely knew me.

"I know you better than you think," he said sedately. "You're my grandson, the son of my own son. I raised your dad. I know the things he would've taught you—even though he removed me from your life ten years ago."

Here was my chance, so I took it. "Why? Why were you removed from my life?"

Grandpa's eyes moistened. "I can't bring myself to tell you, Alan, but you'll find out soon enough."

"How?" I coaxed, not willing to let it go. "How will I find out?"

Grandpa crossed his arms on his chest. Quietly, he said, "The safe contains many valuables—and many answers. It will require some time on your part, but what's in that safe will enlighten you. Since you're stuck here for eight days, give it the time. You'll find out plenty. Maybe too much."

I didn't know what to say. I just stared at my grandfather.

"Go and open the safe," he pressed me. "38-12-33."

I walked around the bed to the five-foot-tall safe. Dropping onto my haunches, I placed my fingers on the gold tumbler combination lock.

"It works just like you'd expect," Grandpa told me. "Right, left, right, bypassing the middle number once."

I spun the dial several times to the right, finally stopping on 38. As I started counterclockwise, I heard the telephone ring in the kitchen. Flustered, I worked the dial past the number 12, then rotated a complete turn to the 12 again. The phone rang a second time.

"Rats!" I grumbled, rising to my feet. Grandpa simply smiled as I ran out of his room. I made it to the phone just as the fourth ring had begun.

"Hello. George Maki's residence," I announced with an irritability I hardly concealed.

"Hello, Alan," my mother's voice greeted me. "I see you made it to Montana, attitude and all."

I smiled into the receiver. "Yes, Mother. Sorry, but we're right in the middle of something."

"Oh? You and who else?"

I leaned my back against the refrigerator. "Me and Santa Claus," I answered in jest, then hurriedly added, "Grandpa." I smiled and hoped my mother was smiling too.

There was a short pause; then she quizzed, "Is everything all right?"

"Things are great; Grandpa's great; I'm great. How'd you get this number? It's not listed."

My mother ignored my question and asked one herself. "Are you sure you're getting along with your grandfather?"

I laughed again. "Mom, is this an inquest? It looks to me like Grandpa and I could've been getting along great for the past ten years, if we'd had the chance."

There was no response for several seconds. Finally she said, "How do you like Montana?"

The rest of our conversation focused on the mundane, and since I was preoccupied with other matters, I sped the call along, hoping to talk more at another time. After heartfelt "I love you's" from each of us, I hung up.

"That was my mom," I informed Grandpa.

He nodded. "Making sure everything's all right."

Smiling, I said, "You know my mom!" As soon as the words left my mouth, I realized I had misspoken.

Grandpa, unconcerned, said kindly, "I just know what good mothers are like, that's all. Good mothers are always making sure everything's OK." He directed me toward the safe.

I went over, squatted, and gazed at the combination lock. I turned it clockwise to 33, then grasped the handle and slowly opened the heavy-gauge steel door.

The first thing I saw inside the safe was a stack of currency that made my eyes bug out. The bill on top was adorned with Benjamin Franklin's picture, making me wonder whether every bill was a hundred.

Lying beside the money was a silver key on a key ring with a hanging gold pendant. The pendant was engraved: *John 3:16*.

"Take the stuff out and put it under the tree," Grandpa said as my eyes focused on a bronzed baby shoe tipped onto its side. I picked up the shoe and stood with it in my hand.

"You should find eight items, not including the papers stashed in the back," Grandpa told me. "Put all of them under the tree."

I dutifully placed the baby shoe on the floor beneath the tree branches, then turned back to the safe. I scooped up the key ring in one hand and snatched a gold-framed certificate with the other. As I laid them beside the shoe, I saw that the certificate was dated 1981 and was from the 8th Annual Skylon International Marathon. My grandfather's name was on it.

"How many have you got out?" Grandpa asked anxiously.

"Three," I said, stepping to the safe. I squatted and peered inside, spotting a double-chained necklace and a folded Santa Claus suit. I took the necklace out first and held it up in front of me.

"Is that the elk-ivory necklace?" wondered Grandpa.

When I told him it was, he said the necklace contained eight bull elk ivories. The creamy-white ivories were inlaid in dangling, stamped silver settings. A large pendant with several turquoise stones surrounding a diamond was also attached to the beaded, silver chains.

"Must be worth a grand," I whispered to myself. Clutching the necklace, I also grabbed the beard and shirt of the Santa costume and deposited the goods under the tree.

"That's five," I notified my grandfather, going back for the black belt and red pants. As I lifted the apparel from the safe, a baseball rolled from beneath the pants and fell onto the floor. It was a hardball that had obviously seen some playing time but nevertheless looked pretty good. I pitched the Santa stuff behind me toward the tree and fielded the baseball.

"Is this the ball you threw that hit me in the nose?" I asked Grandpa.

A wide grin broke across his face. "It has that notoriety, but there's more to it than that."

I held the ball across the seams with my fastball grip. "It's ten-and-a-half years later, so let's see who can catch now!" I said playfully. Grandpa raised his hands as I pretended to throw the ball.

"You missed," he joked, "but it was a good pitch, anyway."

We laughed.

I tidied up the Santa costume and set the baseball on top of the pile. "That makes six," I stated. I looked deeper inside the safe and saw a rifle propped against the back wall beside a heap of papers and manila folders. I grabbed the rifle, and as I drew it out, I looked around for the eighth and last treasure. Other than the papers, the only thing I pinpointed was the money pile.

"I've got the rifle," I announced. The weapon's smooth stock felt perfect in my hands.

"It's a .300 Savage," replied Grandpa, "manufactured in 1962. It's a classic."

I laid the rifle under the tree. "That's seven," I declared. "What's number eight?"

Grandpa rolled his eyes and snickered. "You couldn't possibly have overlooked the hundred-dollar bills, could you?"

I shook my head. I certainly didn't believe he wanted me to fool with his money.

"Take it out and put it under the tree," he said emphatically. "There's ten thousand dollars there, and that's number eight."

Reluctant, I argued, "Shouldn't we leave the money locked in the safe?"

Grandpa flipped a hand toward me. "Nah, just put it under the tree."

His request made little sense, but I took the stack of currency and set it beneath the Christmas tree.

"There!" exclaimed Grandpa with a couple of claps of his hands. "Now we've got some gifts under our tree! Eight gifts, to be exact!"

I gazed at the spread from out of the safe. To say the least, I was definitely interested in the history behind each item.

"OK, close the safe, Alan; don't forget the combination."

After a final glance inside at the mysterious papers, I

placed the flat of my hand against the steel door and pushed it shut. Grabbing the handle, I jerked it upward, securing the catch. Lastly I spun the dial. The safe was locked.

Chapter Five

The Choice Presented

I wanted to hear about the objects under the tree, but the excitement of opening the safe had been too much for Grandpa.

"Just let me sleep for a little while," he said, closing his eyes. "We'll talk later tonight."

I took a minute to reset my watch from 7:45 to 5:45 P.M.

"You got a TV, Grandpa?"

Without opening his eyes, he answered, "No, but there's a portable radio in the top left dresser drawer. Can't get many stations though. This isn't Ann Arbor."

I opened the drawer and took out the small radio. I also picked up the tray of dirty dishes, flicked off the bedroom light, and went into the kitchen. After playing for a minute with the radio dial, I found KLYQ broadcasting light rock music from Hamilton.

I took a few minutes to wash the dishes, then found a bag of dog food in the kitchen pantry. I scooped out a nice ration for Buck. Then I filled a teakettle with cold tap water.

"Bu-u-uck!" I called as I walked down the back porch steps. The light shining through the kitchen window enabled me to find the dog's dishes in the darkness. I filled the bowls and went back into the house.

For something to do, I began looking through the front of the house for some reading material. Finding nothing, it dawned on me that all the books were on Grandpa's bookshelves in his bedroom.

"Great," I grumbled, not wanting to spend the next hour just twiddling my thumbs. I decided to sneak into Grandpa's room to get a good book to read.

The farther I walked down the hallway, the less light I had, and I realized I wouldn't be able to see in the bedroom. I entered the room regardless and was met by the sound of Grandpa's soft snoring. Tiptoeing in the dark, I groped for the rows of books against the wall.

"I need night vision," I mumbled, unable to make out any titles. Stymied, I took a chance and simply plucked three books off a shelf. I retreated to the dining room and sat down at the table before checking my luck.

The fattest book was a paperback entitled *The International Thesaurus of Quotations*, which I thought might be interesting for fifteen or twenty minutes. Another paperback, *Robert's Rules of Order*, was not interesting for even fifteen seconds. I was left with high hopes for the third book, a thin hardcover whose title, *Old Kalevala*, gave no secrets away to me. I cracked open the book and began reading, enjoying the music from the radio too.

Over the next hour I found *Old Kalevala* to be less than stimulating, but I read enough to get the gist of it. The book contained Finnish folklore concerning a man named Vainamoinen. He built ships, sailed the seas making war, and was so lucky that arrows wouldn't pierce his clothing. Vainamoinen's sword was longer than anyone else's, and he fought the Lapps and cut off a lot of heads.

I discovered that finally a Lapp shot Vainamoinen's horse over the surface of the sea with a crossbow, causing Vainamoinen to fall into the water, where he drifted for years. Then, as he floated in one place, an eagle from the land of Finmark made a nest on him and laid six golden eggs and a seventh of iron. When Vainamoinen moved, the eggs rolled into the water and smashed into bits. The upper part of the shells formed the heavens, while the lower part formed the rest of the earth. The white of the eggs changed into the sun. The yolk formed into the moon, and all the other pieces were changed into stars and scattered into space.

"Yeah, right," I chuckled, closing the book. "And then Vainamoinen climbed out of the water as a shriveled up prune, with skin desperately in need of some heavy-duty hand lotion."

Laughing out loud at my own sarcasm, I got up and browsed around the kitchen for snack ideas. I found graham crackers, peanuts, Pop Tarts, and cornflakes in the cupboards, and celery, carrots, apples, orange juice, and Pepsi in the refrigerator, all of which looked good to me.

Unable to abstain until Grandpa awoke, I took the can of peanuts and a can of pop back to the dining room table. Then I picked up the book of quotations. It fell open to a section titled "Life." Seven pages were devoted to notable quotes about that particular subject, followed by three more pages titled "Life and Death." Several of the quotes had been underlined with ink, so I read them.

"Life is half spent before one knows what life is," read a French proverb.

Edgar Lee Masters had written, "It takes life to love Life."

"Life is the external text, the burning bush by the edge of the path from which God speaks," wrote José Ortega y Gasset.

"Our life is made by the death of others," penned Leonardo da Vinci.

Mark Twain wrote, "Oh Death where is thy sting! It has none. But life has."

Intrigued by these selections, I assumed my grandfather had been the one who had marked them. I pondered for a moment what was on his mind, and that gave me a thought. Flipping pages backward, I turned to the "Ds." Sure enough, in the category titled "Death," I found three quotations underlined.

"He hath lived ill that knows not how to die well," said the first.

"Do not seek death. Death will find you. But seek the road which makes death a fulfillment," read the second.

The third was doubly emphasized. "Death surprises us in the midst of our hopes."

I closed the book and leaned back in my chair. At that moment, the fact that my grandfather was actually dying hit me hard. Until then, his existence had been acknowledged though disregarded by me and everyone else who was important to me. But suddenly reality sank in. I had less than eight days to spend with this engaging man. Then I would go home, and he would go dead. And everything he knew that was worth knowing would go dead with him.

I looked at my watch. It was almost 7:30. I clicked off the radio and headed for Grandpa's bedroom. Entering his darkened room, I heard him stirring.

"Grandpa?"

"I'm awake. Turn on the light."

I flipped the switch.

"Would you do me a favor, Alan?" Grandpa asked, grabbing his Bible and eyeglasses off the teak end table. He set his glasses on his lap and slipped a small booklet from out of the Bible. Tossing the booklet to me, he asked, "Would you read today's devotional from *Our Daily Bread*?"

Feeling uncomfortable but trying not to show it, I looked at the cover photograph of a huge arch of red rock. Beneath the picture were the words, "The Lord lives! Blessed be my Rock! Let God be exalted, the Rock of my salvation!" I knew I was in for some kind of religious instruction, and I wasn't sure I wanted any. But in spite of my emotions, I respectfully turned to the reading for Saturday, December 16, which was titled "Purge Out the Poison." I was happy to find that the devotional consisted of only four short paragraphs.

"Got it?"

"Yes," I replied, thinking this might be easy after all—then I began reading aloud. I made it only into the second paragraph before conviction surprised me and stung my conscience.

One portion read, "Bitterness is a poison, and if not purged out by prayer, confession, and forgiveness, it does great emotional damage and destroys relationships. A little grudge that festers can become a devastating malignancy of the soul."

I stopped reading and stared at Grandpa. He smiled and encouraged, "Good stuff. Keep going."

I looked back at the words "Have you been holding fast to the memory of some insult, some event, some criticism?" I read, thinking about the separation between my family and my grandfather. I sensed Grandpa was thinking the same thing, but I continued reading: "Take the proper steps to resolve the problem right away. Holding a grudge poisons our spiritual lives. With the Holy Spirit's help, let's uproot any bitterness right now." I closed the booklet and dropped it on the edge of the bed.

Grandpa was ready for me. His Bible was open, and his eyeglasses sat on his nose. He recited, "Bear with each other and forgive whatever grievances you may have against one another. Forgive as the Lord forgave you."

He took off his glasses and gazed at me. "What do you think?" he questioned, letting his Bible fall shut.

"What do I think?" I repeated, recognizing that my grandfather had once again put me on the spot. I threw the ball back to him: "About what?"

"About forgiveness," he announced. It was a topic far bigger than I had expected.

Chickening out, I shrugged.

My grandfather's face registered disappointment, but he quickly smiled and let me off the hook. Resting his hands on his Bible, he said softly, "God is a forgiving God, Alan, and we should be forgiving too. Understand?"

I understood only that Grandpa had just hit me over the head with his religion. I thought I'd smack him back with another "religion."

Keeping a straight face, I said, "What about Vainamoinen and the eagle eggs?"

Grandpa's eyebrows rose in surprise, then he burst out laughing. I laughed with him until he started coughing, which gave me pause; then he cracked up again.

"Vainamoinen?" he blurted. "He's a wannabe god! You've read the *Kalevala*?"

"Yeah, while you were sleeping."

Chuckling, Grandpa remarked, "Finnish folklore is fun, I suppose, but it sure stretches the imagination." He shook his head, then grew serious.

I cringed. "What is it?"

He looked toward our Christmas tree, mulling something over in his mind. "There are eight gifts over there," he acknowledged.

I sat still, awaiting his punch line.

"I want you to make a choice," Grandpa stated, stressing the final word.

"What?" I prodded him.

Tucking his hands under his blanket, he said, "I want you to choose one gift from the eight for yourself, but not until the day you go home, which is your birthday." He watched my face for understanding. When he saw my blank stare, he reiterated, "One of the items is yours, but you can't decide until your birthday. Then you can take any one you want."

I felt my heart speed up. "Really?" I exclaimed, looking at the things beneath the tree.

"It's your choice," my grandfather repeated, "so think about it."

I could almost smell the money from my chair.

Chapter Six

The Stories

I stayed in Grandpa's room for another hour, snacking on graham crackers and milk. I told my grandfather about my baseball career, which delighted him, and he spoke at length of his move to Montana after his retirement in 1989. When nine o'clock rolled around, the effects of jet lag hit me.

"I've got to crash," I told my grandpa, slumping in my chair. "Do you want anything before I go?"

Grandpa nodded toward the dresser. "It's time for two pills. Lasix and Inderal."

I got up and examined the four pill bottles sitting on the dresser top.

"Lasix is white and Inderal's a gold tablet," Grandpa helped me. As I fought with the childproof caps, he said, "Digoxin's white, too, and Procardia's a gold capsule. I need all four at nine tomorrow morning."

"You sound like a pharmacist," I kidded.

"Yes," he agreed with a laugh, "but I feel like a drug

addict." I gave him the two tablets and watched as he drank them down with his milk. I then gathered the dishes we had used that evening.

"Where does Buck sleep?" I asked.

"He has the run of the house. He'll usually come in here or lie down by the stove." Grinning, he added, "Who knows? Maybe he'll want to sleep with you."

I forced a smile. "We'll see."

"Put two of the bigger logs on the fire. That'll do for the night. And don't worry about me. I'll holler if I need you."

"OK, Grandpa. You want the light out?"

"Not yet. After you get ready for bed, come back and flick the switch for me."

I left his room and set the dirty dishes in the kitchen sink, then found Buck outside by the woodpile. I grabbed two logs and took them, along with the dog, into the house. Buck trotted to his master's bedroom while I fueled the fire in the stove.

After washing up in the nauseous pink bathroom, I slipped into a pair of blue-plaid pajamas I had brought with me. I walked toward my grandfather's bedroom to turn out the light. From the hallway I saw that his room was already dark. I heard a quiet voice. His voice. Curious, I tiptoed to the bedroom door and listened.

"...and please, Lord, take me home soon. Don't let me linger and be a burden on anyone. I'm grateful I've lived long enough to see this day, a day on which I've seen my grandson. Thank you for the love he's shown me, love I can feel despite all the lost years. Bless him and make his heart soft.

"I also pray for my son, Dale, and his wife, Nancy. I pray that Dale would...would...forgive...."

I didn't move an inch as my grandfather sobbed.

"God, please help Dale," he said between heaves, "and give me courage to hold fast till the end, that I might die well. Amen."

Hugging the hallway wall, I escaped to the dining room, turned off the lights in the house, and went into my bedroom. I threw myself onto the bed, which was akin to plunging into foam rubber quicksand. The springs creaked and pinged as I sank down. I started to get angry, but chose to laugh instead.

Drawn by the commotion, Buck walked in and stuck his nose in my face. I gently pushed him away, covered my head with the blanket, and went to sleep.

I awoke the next morning at 5:45, which was early for most everyone in Montana on a Sunday, but my inner time clock hadn't yet reset itself. I clambered off my spongy mattress in the dark, sensing a dull ache in my lower back.

"Great," I grumbled, rubbing the painful area with my hand. I turned on the ceiling light and gave the bed a disdainful look as though it might understand. Buck, lying at the foot of the bed, looked at me with sleepy eyes and didn't bother to get up.

After using the bathroom, I unpacked my bags and put on a pair of jeans, a Michigan sweatshirt, and my sneakers.

I let Buck outside and fed the fire. Then I sat down at the dining room table.

"Good morning, Alan." I jumped at the sound of my grandfather's voice. He walked around me to the opposite side of the table, looking rested and younger than the previous day.

"You look pretty good this morning," I complimented him.

He sat down, grinning. "I believe seeing you has put some vitality back into me, so I've decided to live a little longer!"

"That's the right attitude," I replied happily. "How 'bout some orange juice to boost your energy?"

"OK," he agreed, and I slowly got up.

Grandpa, noticing my laggard pace, asked, "How'd you sleep?"

"Could've been better."

"Bed too hard?" he asked knowingly.

I laughed. "Yeah, too hard on my back." I took two glasses from the cupboard and filled them with juice. "Don't worry, I'll get used to the bed."

"You're dreaming!" Grandpa laughed.

I came back to the table with the drinks. Grandpa stared thoughtfully at me as I sat down.

"I gather your parents have never told you why they left me out of their lives, and out of your life."

I nodded. "That's right. They've totally avoided the topic."

A look of sadness swept over him. "That really bothers me." He patted my outstretched hand, then took a drink of juice and cleared his throat.

"It's not right for me to go to my grave without you knowing the truth." He studied my face with his piercing blue eyes. I stared back, hungering for more information.

Breaking the silence I asked, "Are you gonna tell me?"

He shook his head. "No, I'm not going to tell you, 'cause it's too painful for me, but I'm going to have you read about it."

"Read about it?" I blurted. "Where?"

Grandpa took a breath and rattled off, "38-12-33." Then he drank some more juice.

My thoughts raced. I remembered the stack of papers and manila folders in the back of the safe.

"The story's in the safe?" I asked.

Putting down his glass, he said, "There are eight stories in the safe, Alan. One for every item under the Christmas tree." He waited for me to nod my head before adding, "I want you to get them out and read them, and you'll find that one of them explains the hurt between your dad and me. All eight of them explain parts of my life and the significance of the gifts, and they'll help you decide which one to choose."

I shoved my chair away from the table and stood up, anxious to get my hands on the stories. "You wrote them?"

"Yes," said my grandfather. "They're sitting on top, each in its own folder and marked according to the gift it represents."

"Gotcha!" I made haste to Grandpa's bedroom. I went straight to the safe, where I worked the combination and opened the door. I reached inside and grabbed the top pack of manila folders.

Encouraged, I secured the door and stood up with my find. Each folder held several pages and was titled on the front in black ink. The top one read, "Baseball." The second, "Baby Shoe." The third, "Silver Key," and so on. I remembered my grandfather telling me the safe contained many valuables and many answers. I never suspected those answers might come in story form.

I got the feeling the words would impress me.

Chapter Seven

The Baseball

As Grandpa and I ate cereal and toast, I could hardly keep my thoughts off the eight manila folders I had set on the table. Grandpa spoke about ice fishing on a lake somewhere, but he could tell my mind was preoccupied, so he changed his subject.

"About those stories," he said between spoonfuls of cereal, "there's a catch to your reading them."

My attention captured, I asked eagerly, "What is it?"

He looked me in the eye. "You may read only two of the stories a day. It'll take four days to get through them all."

Befuddled by the directive, I made a silly face. "Why?"

"I want you to take your time. There's a lot of emotion involved. You'll see some of my heartaches, and I don't want the weight of it to hit you all at once. There's much to digest."

I couldn't believe his request. I had missed out on knowing my grandfather for the past ten-and-a-half years, and now that I had my hands on narratives that would help fill in the void, he was asking me to shilly-shally around.

Unable to hide my disgruntlement, I said, "Come on, Grandpa! I could read them all today!"

He shook his head and held his ground. "No, I want you to give it more time. We haven't shared our lives week by week over the past decade like many grandparents and grandchildren. I can't just drop ten years' worth of stuff on you in one day. Let's go slowly so you and I can make it through—together." He took a bite of cereal. "Humor me," he spoke between crunches.

I was thwarted, but I couldn't get mad at my grandpa. He grinned goofily at me, and I responded with a compulsory smile.

"No one else has ever seen these stories," he said, once again serious. "Alan, I want you to burn them after you're through."

"Burn them?" I choked out, ever amazed by the old man's thinking.

He stood up from the table, disregarding my reaction. "I'm going back to my room for a while." Walking away, he said, "Go ahead and read two of the stories. Any two you want. I know you're chomping at the bit. And may God help us." With that, he disappeared down the hallway, and I reached for the top manila folder.

Pushing my breakfast dishes aside, I opened the folder and fingered the typed, single-spaced pages titled "Baseball." Since that hardball lying beneath the Christmas tree had seemingly finalized our family split, I thought reading about the ball would be the best place to look for answers. I laid the story out before me and began soaking up every word.

6/21/92

I love baseball. When I was a kid, I loved baseball even more. As a matter of fact, baseball was the most important thing in my life until I was 18 years old. I played ball all day long in the spring and summer with the neighborhood kids, and when the kids went home, I practiced pitching at a tire for hours by myself. Yes, I really loved baseball.

When I was 12 years old and in Little League, I was an all-star pitcher. The first game of the year was a good one for me; I hurled a no-hitter and struck out 13 batters. My team won, 7-0. In my second start, I pitched a four-hitter and won, 2-0. My brother Leonard was my catcher in both of those games, and he did a tremendous job behind the plate; he was an all-star catcher.

I was winning my third game by a 7-0 score going into the last inning, and the coach put a substitute catcher into the ball game. He was giving the second-string catcher some playing time in a game that was obviously "in the bag." I didn't think twice about the move. All I was thinking about was getting three outs and recording my third straight shutout.

With two outs and only one to go, the opposing team's best and biggest player reached first base. I don't remember how he got there. What I do remember is that the next batter hit a ball into center field. To my amazement, the runner on first not only didn't stop at second base, but he didn't stop at third. He was trying to score all the way from first base on a single to center! He was going to ruin my shutout!

I cut off the throw from the center fielder at the pitcher's mound and eyed the galloping lead runner. I almost laughed to myself for a split second, thinking all I had to do was flip the ball to my brother and the foolish runner would be dead meat at home plate. I spun and brought my right arm back to throw the ball; at that instant, I saw and remembered that my brother wasn't at home plate. The second-string, smaller catcher was there, anxiously awaiting my throw.

"No way," I thought. "No way will I throw the ball to that kid. He'll drop the ball, and I'll lose my shutout. Instead, I'll tag out the runner myself."

I ran into the base path in front of home plate, and the base runner ran into me. We collided with great force, and I was knocked to the ground. The air was knocked out of me, and I lay in the dirt, squirming. But I still had the ball, and the runner was out.

I hadn't thrown the ball to the second-string catcher because I didn't trust him to handle the putout at the plate. I trusted only myself. And since I kept the ball myself, that meant I had to handle the collision myself. There was no one to help me handle the shock. I was on my own.

I've thought a lot about that day when I kept the ball to myself, and I've often applied my old baseball stories to my present-day life.

I've got another All-Star Catcher to help me now. It's not my brother Leonard anymore because he lives in Florida, and that's a long toss from Darby, Montana. No, my All-Star Catcher is God. When I trust God and throw the ball to him, he handles the collisions. He is the sturdy rock crouched over home plate. He makes the play.

How do I throw the ball to God? Through prayer. I talk to him about my impending collisions and put my life in his hands. When I trust God, I feel a sense of security and confidence.

I like the peace that overwhelms me when I know that God is watching over me. I like throwing the ball to God because he has saved many shutouts for me.

Believe me, God is an All-Star Catcher.

At this point there was a quarter-of-a-page gap before the beginning of the next paragraph, so I stopped reading. I relished what I had read of my grandfather's pitching prowess, and I mused over his playing catch with God. I deduced I must have received my pitching genes from him, and I wondered if there was a religious gene.

Looking again to the story, I continued reading.

I took home the baseball I had kept to myself. My coach gave it to me, and my father locked it in his safe for me as a keepsake. The ball remained in the safe for the next forty-two years, rarely touched or even mentioned.

Then one day in June of 1985, a little boy stood dejectedly in my backyard, crying over the loss of his new baseball. It seemed that someone had stolen it.

Since that boy was my grandson, his loss felt like my loss, and his tears were my tears. I went to my father's safe, which was now my safe, and found the well-preserved baseball from my own playing days. Happily, I gave the ball as a gift to the little fellow and stopped his many tears. His countenance turned to joy.

My trembling hand dropped the typed page on the table. I sat in stunned silence, knowing where this story was heading. I had been at the end of this tale in real life, and I needed to brace myself to go there again.

Getting up, I carried my juice glass to the kitchen sink and poured the remaining liquid down the drain. I filled the glass with tap water and took a drink, then sucked in a deep breath and walked back to the table.

"*...much to digest,*" my grandfather's words banged in my head. I sat down and grittily picked up the story where I had left off.

As I started back to the house, my grandson ran after me, pleading, "Grandpa! Play catch with me! Please?"

I looked into his eager eyes and saw myself at the same age of nine, hunting down my father or my grandfather or anyone at all who would spare the time to toss a ball with me. And if Alan's eyes weren't enough to draw me, the alluring sound of the ball popping into my grandson's well-oiled glove was, as he played catch with himself while waiting for my answer.

"You betcha!" I responded with a big grin, and I retrieved a dusty old mitt from my backyard shed.

For the next fifteen minutes, grandfather and grandson did what grandfathers and grandsons had been doing for decades. The grandson tried as hard as he could to fire the ball as fast as lightning, and the grandpa tossed it back as gently as a freshly laid egg.

"Throw it harder, Grandpa!" begged the kid. "I'm not a baby! I can catch!"

I acquiesced and put a little more steam on my throws, and sure enough, the boy could catch. Each time he snagged the ball out of the air, he smiled proudly, fired it back, and beckoned for more.

This kid is special, I thought. Winding up, I threw one a little harder.

The truth is, anyone can make a mistake, and anyone can misjudge a ball. I made the mistake and Alan misjudged, and my fastball nipped the top of his glove and was brought to a stop by his face. Blood spurted out of his nose, tears streamed out of his eyes, and his parents raced out of the house.

The last words I heard from my grandson's father, Dale, were, "This is the last straw! Because of you, our family's been ruined!" The car door slammed, and no one looked back as the car drove away, except Alan. Peering above a blood-soaked towel held to his nose were those sorrowful blue eyes. I wanted to wave good-bye, but my arms were dead at my sides. Anyway, I was sure this was temporary anger and my family would be back soon.

Later, in my backyard, I found the baseball I had given my grandson lying in the grass. I picked it up and wiped off some blood. The ball had been mine, but now it was Alan's, and I would save it for him until he came by again with eyes eager for a game of catch with his grandfather. I loved that little boy, and I couldn't wait to make things right and give him a hug.

The sad thing is that seven years have come and gone since that day in my backyard. My grandson

has never come back, the hug has never been ex-
changed, my family has remained cold, and I have
grown old waiting.

As for the baseball, I cradle it in my hands once
in a while, remembering the good old days, the no-
hitters, the shutouts, and my grandson.

I fell back in my chair and burst into tears. My heart
was crushed inside my chest. Never had I been so moved
by any man's writing as this, and I dropped my head in
humility and shame, thinking of the pain that my grandfather, my own flesh and blood, had endured. How he
had mustered the strength to put this story on paper, I
couldn't imagine. And I knew deep within, like he had
written, my tears were his tears.

How can I ever face my grandpa again? I wondered,
whipping myself with my thoughts. I believed I had
single-handedly ruined the last decade of his life.

"Alan?" came my grandfather's voice from behind me.

I quickly wiped my eyes. Without turning around, I
uttered, "Yes?"

"You were just a kid." His hand clasped my shoulder.
"It's not your fault." There was a pause as he let his soft-
ly spoken words resound in my mind; then he repeated,
"It's not your fault, son."

I caught my breath and held it fast, rose to my feet,
and faced Grandpa. He, too, was crying.

"How 'bout that hug?" he choked.

I buried my face in his shoulder.

Patting my back, Grandpa whispered, "Everything's
all right now." His arms squeezed me tighter, and I was
lifted by his love.

Chapter Eight

Robin and the Rifle

The baseball story, though it filled in some blanks, didn't get directly to the bottom of things. Grandpa encouraged me to remain patient and keep reading, but I wasn't ready for the task. Having cried more in the last ten minutes than I had in all of the past ten years, I thought I might die from dehydration should I immediately read another tear-jerking story.

Needing a break, I asked my grandfather if I could take a drive in my car. "We're out of milk, so I'll buy some in Darby."

"Mr. T's will be open," he told me.

"Been there," I declared, slipping into my jacket. "You'll be all right for about fifteen minutes?"

He showed me the small radio in his hand. "I'm going to my bedroom to listen to a church service."

"OK, I'll be back shortly."

The Taurus started without hesitation, even though the air temperature couldn't have been above ten degrees, and I headed for town. Just a mile and a half from Grandpa's house I spotted a "Historic Point" sign and pulled into a turnoff beside two wooden markers. Both of them cited information about Trapper Peak, a wonderfully jagged, snow-capped granite mountain I could see in the distance.

"At 10,157 feet in elevation," one sign read, "magnificent Trapper Peak rises higher than any other peak in the 200-mile-long Bitterroot Mountain Range that extends along the Idaho-Montana border from the Snake River Valley in Idaho to the Clark Fork River in Montana. The Range includes howling wilderness, yawning canyons, and towering mountains covered with a heavy growth of pine and fir."

The second sign cited the history of the spot: "In 1805, members of the Lewis and Clark Expedition passed here, followed by traders, trappers, and missionaries. In an attempt to flee from the U.S. Army in 1877, the non-treaty Nez Perce Native Americans passed peacefully through the Valley on their way east." The last sentence inspired me: "Trapper Peak's timeless and sturdy form represents history; from the historic travelers of the past, to the modern-day travelers of tomorrow."

I admired the peaks jabbing into the arctic blue sky, glad for the sight but just as glad for a warm car and the fact that I wasn't trapped somewhere on Trapper Peak.

Steering the car back onto the highway, I drove the three remaining miles along the Bitterroot River to Darby and Mr. T's. My heart leaped when I saw the sports car with the "PSALM 1" license plate parked in front of the store.

I went inside, looking for Robin Patterson. I found her browsing in an aisle with a gallon of milk in her hand.

"We've got to quit meeting like this," she joked.

Looking for something to say, I pointed at her milk jug. "That's what I'm here for," I said awkwardly.

"Oh, well, there's plenty more over there," she giggled, nodding toward the back of the store.

"I didn't mean I wanted yours! I just meant...oh, you know what I meant." I flushed with embarrassment and followed Robin to the front counter.

"I'm on my way to church," she explained, "but my dad needed some milk for his breakfast. My parents aren't feeling well, so I'm going to church alone."

I wondered whether Robin was giving me an opening to invite myself along or if I simply possessed a vivid imagination. Assuming the latter, I passed on making a pass. Instead, I stood mum while she paid for the milk.

"Actually," she said, preparing to leave, "I had planned on visiting George this afternoon, but since you're here, I guess he's not hurting for company."

I moved toward the door with her, digging fast for the right words. "Um...ah," I started poorly. I poked my hands into my jacket pockets. "Please stop by. It'll brighten his day." I held the door as Robin left the store.

Looking back, she said, "I'll try to make it around three."

"OK," I said, letting her go. I purchased some milk of my own and drove back to my grandfather's house, happy as a lark.

When I walked through the front door, Buck charged through the house to meet me. He trailed me to the kitchen, then to Grandpa's room. I heard the radio blaring, and when I looked in the bedroom, I saw my grandfather sitting up in bed with his eyes closed. He was wearing the nasal cannula and I could see his chest moving, so I knew he was all right. I couldn't tell whether he was sleeping or concentrating on the man preaching over the radio, but either way, he was content.

I moved to the dining room, slipped off my jacket, and sat down. Buck, sticking with me, lay down at my feet beneath the table. I picked up the stack of manila folders and shuffled through them, endeavoring to put Robin out of my mind. I took out the stories titled "Money" and "The Rifle." Perhaps one of those would provide more details concerning my parents' alienation from my grandfather. Since people had been known to kill for money, with a rifle often the weapon of choice, I figured I was on the right track.

Saving "Money" for the next day, I opened the other folder and lifted the top page. Glassy-eyed, I gazed at the paper but visualized only Robin's face smiling at me. I caught myself stupidly smiling back.

Snapping out of it, I narrowed my eyes and focused on the story at hand.

12/12/91

I stopped by Uncle Mack's home to pick him up to go deer hunting for the last time. I didn't know then that it was the last time, but it was. I knocked on the front door, which had the Finnish word Kaukomieli freshly painted on it.

"Man with a far-roving mind," I translated aloud, chuckling at its appropriateness.

"Come on in!" Mack screeched from inside. I opened the door and entered the cozy living room.

"Yep. I'm ready to go," Mack announced as he came through his bedroom door, smiling. His face

was tawny and wrinkled like a paper bag that had been used over and over again; it was a face I loved.

Mack carried his faded blue tote bag in one crinkled, bony hand and his encased rifle in the other.

"Grab my boots and coat, George, and let's go." We walked out of the house and into a long-awaited week.

For a dozen years, it had been this way. Always on November 14, which was the day before deer-hunting season opened in Michigan, I picked up Mack and we drove more than three hundred miles to a small, two-story cabin north of Escanaba.

As was our custom, when we reached Manistique, we patronized a sauna house. Inside the sauna room, Mack slopped water onto the heated rocks in a sunken furnace, then sat naked next to me on the lacquered bench as the rocks hissed like angry snakes.

I breathed deeply the dry heat vapors while staring dreamily at the sign hanging above the door: "All Your Cares Float Away."

"Yep. This must be what heaven is like," Mack said.

Twenty minutes later we were back in the car, heading for the cabin. Mack sat in the passenger seat with his head tilted back.

"There's nothing like a good sauna," he said softly. A smile tugged at the corners of his mouth. "You know, George, during all the wars with Russia, the Finn soldiers couldn't go without their sauna. Why, when the Finns advanced into Russia, they built a sauna during every rest period. Then they left a soldier behind to keep the sauna hot for when they retreated."

Almost before I was done laughing, Mack was snoring.

* * *

As dusk settled over the land, the roads I drove became narrower and the houses got farther and farther apart. We were but a couple of miles from the cabin when a white Lincoln Continental pulled out in front of me from an obscured driveway, and I slammed on the brake pedal. Mack pitched forward, popping open his eyes and grabbing the dashboard.

"Crazy driver!" I thundered, my heart pounding from the scare.

Mack, too, was having a heart problem. He clutched at his chest.

"You OK?" I questioned.

"Yep. Just having a heart attack, is all."

I gazed at my uncle, who wasn't smiling. "Are you serious?"

"Almost," he whimpered.

Suddenly a whitetail deer jumped out of the ditch on the driver's side and leaped into the road. I hit my brakes again. The other driver did not react fast enough; his vehicle slammed into the deer, knocking the animal down.

I stopped my car short of the fallen deer and watched the Lincoln drive off.

"He's not even going to stop!" Mack shouted as he opened the passenger door. I got out and stood beside my uncle, looking at the dying deer.

"He's just a little button buck," Mack whispered. He knelt down by the deer's head and lightly touched one ear. The deer shuddered.

Buck broke my concentration by getting up and trotting to the back door of the house. He scratched the door twice with his paw, yearning to go outdoors. I put the story on the table and took care of the dog.

While I was up, I grabbed a can of Pepsi from the fridge. Cracking open the top, I took a swig and found my place in the story.

"You're bleeding, little fella," Mack said, looking at the bloody snow. He gently stroked the deer's forehead. Its breath curled up in Mack's face.

"It's not fair you had to go like this," Mack spoke softly. "That Lincoln Continental doesn't belong out here in the woods. You belong here, and I love it out here like you do. That's why I'm glad I can be with you now. We belong out here."

The deer's body quivered for a few more seconds, then the deer died and the shaking stopped.

Mack rose to his feet. "Let's call the game warden from the next house."

As we walked back to the car, I draped an arm around my uncle's shoulders. It was just a little gesture to tell him that I loved him.

Later, when we arrived at the cabin, Stig, Martti, and Jeff greeted us at the front door.

"Paiva," Mack said, which means hello in Finnish.

"Hey, bloods!" welcomed Martti, hugging his Uncle Mack and Cousin George.

"Ja, how ya doin', boys?" Stig, the Swedish owner of the cabin, shook our hands.

As we took chairs, Jeff, who was Martti's friend,

said he was glad to see us again. This was our second time at the cabin with Jeff.

"Ya ready ta hunt in da mornin'?" Stig asked us, his Swedish accent sounding good to my ears.

"Mack's ready," offered Martti. "Didn't you notice the blood on his pants? Looks like he's already bagged his buck!"

Mack shook his head solemnly. "It was a buck, all right, but the little fella never had a chance." Then Mack went ahead and told the story.

Afterward, Martti served everyone coffee.

"We'll drive dat liddle woods ta da sout' of us first ting in da mornin'," Stig said, sipping his drink. "Dat's always good fer at least one buck. Mack an' Martti can post da east an' west sides of da woods, an' Jeff can watch da sout' end. George an' I will ziggyzag in da woods an' chase out da deer."

With that finalized, I emptied my car of gear and went upstairs in the cabin to bed. I was asleep before anyone else ascended the stairs.

"Git up! It's time ta hunt." I awoke to Stig's shouting.

"What time is it?" I grouched.

"Daylight in da swamp. Time ta hunt."

As the skies brightened, Martti, Jeff, and Mack piled into Stig's old Jeep. They were going to drive a half mile to the opposite end of the woods that Stig and I would walk through. Mack would be dropped off on the west side of the woods while Jeff would park the Jeep and post himself at the southern end. Martti would walk around to the east side and cover numerous deer trails that ran in and out of the woods.

"I'll chase 'em your way, Uncle!" I hollered at Mack through the Jeep window.

"That's my boy!" he proclaimed, his paper-bag face folding into a big grin. The Jeep rolled away, and I watched Mack's head, covered with an orange, pullover wool hat, bobbing up and down with every dip the vehicle took. It looked like an orange fishing bobber, bouncing on ripples in a stream, and I laughed at the action.

"Let's start fer da woods," Stig said when the Jeep disappeared. I grabbed my rifle and followed Stig across a snow-covered meadow to the edge of the woods the two of us would drive.

"I'll take the west half," I told the Swede.

"Ja," was all he said in reply as he took off toward the east.

When Stig was fifty yards away from me, I stepped into the woods. I began breaking off branches to make noise as I moved through the trees. Stig hollered "whoop" periodically as he walked off to my left.

I found a good deer trail to walk along, and in a spot where the snow was not very deep, I noticed the fresh track of a big deer. A second later, a wiry branch hit me squarely in the right eye. I fell to my knees, set my rifle against a tree, and threw off my gloves.

"Crud," I muttered, rubbing my injured eye. Tears spilled out, and the eyelids squeezed shut.

I picked up my gloves and gun. Climbing to my feet, I trotted along the deer trail with one eye open and one eye closed.

After stumbling along for a couple hundred yards, I heard a crash in front of me. I strained to see flashes *of a whitetail deer running away. Making out the un-mistakable gleam of antlers, I brought up my rifle, but when I looked down the barrel with my right eye, everything was a blur.*

I lowered the rifle, disgusted with my poor luck.

"What was dat?" Stig called from a distance.

"A buck!" I yelled. "Mack'll get him!" The deer had gone straight south, then veered to the west toward the road where Mack was posted.

As my eye recovered, I walked the next seventy-five yards anticipating Mack's rifle report, but it never came.

"Stig!" I shouted. "I'm going out to the road to see why Mack didn't shoot! Wait for me!"

"Ja!" came the reply.

I walked in the deer tracks, which took me out of the woods to the road. I looked off in a southerly direction for my uncle. I couldn't see him at first, so I walked down the road a ways until I spied his orange hat.

"Hey!" I yelled and waved an arm in the air.

There was no response.

Hurrying closer, I saw my uncle's posture was slumped. His rifle was lying in the snow at his feet.

"Mack!" I screamed. The moment I reached his side, I knew my uncle was dead. His face was blue and his eyes were glazed. I saw death in his blank stare.

I dropped my own rifle in the snow, pulled off my gloves, and searched Mack's wrist for a pulse.

"Oh, God," I cried, falling to my knees. I wrapped my arms around my uncle. "Why now?" I whimpered.

I tipped my head back and looked up at the sky between two treetops. The branches above me quivered back and forth in the wind, and beyond them I saw a lone hawk gliding across the gray clouds. I blinked to clear away the tears.

Mack's words flooded my brain. "You belong here, and I love it out here like you do. That's why I'm glad I can be with you now. We belong out here."

I hugged Mack's head tighter to my chest.

"This is where you'd have wanted to die," I whispered, trying more than anything else to console myself. My mouth was just an inch from the old Finn's ear. "I love you, Uncle Mack. I love you!"

The sound of Martti's gun echoed in the distance.

I jumped up from my chair and walked to the kitchen, despite the fact there was a bit more to read. I opened the back door and stepped outside into the cold, determined not to let the story get to me.

Buck trotted around the back of the barn, saw me, and came to the porch.

"Good boy," I said, stroking the hair on Buck's back. "You love it out here, don't you, fella?" I looked out at the beautiful acreage before me. "You belong here." Realizing I was quoting words from my grandfather's story, I shook my head at myself.

"He got me again," I muttered. I snatched two logs from the woodpile and went back inside the house. I fed the fire, then sat down to finish the reading.

I resurrected Mack's rifle from the snow and brushed it off. Mack had told me the year before that upon his death he wanted me to have the .300 Savage. I had shrugged him off at the time, telling him he'd probably live another thirty years and outlive me. Little did I know his death was fast approaching.

That's the way death is. It comes when it comes. When it's time, it's time. Ready or not. Death strips you bare on the face of this earth. Every item you thought you owned becomes somebody else's property. And so it was with Uncle Mack's rifle; it now belonged to me, at least for a little while. It was a treasure I would cherish until my hunting days came to a close. Then, Lord willing, I'd be granted a moment to give it to another worthy man who would value the rifle for yet a little while longer.

In this manner, a gun may "live on" forever. And so may a man, as he passes out of the hands of loved ones on earth and into the hands of God.

I look forward to the day when I'll meet my Maker. I'm hoping it will be on a glorious day in a glorious place surrounded by people I love, as with Uncle Mack. In the meantime, I'll keep an eye out for the special man to whom I'll give a special gun.

I placed the pages in the manila folder and set the folder on top of the others. Emotionally spent by the content of the first two stories, I decided to forgo any additional reading for the day, as Grandpa had requested.

"Grandpa knows best," I said to myself. I crossed my arms on the table and lay my head down on my arms. I slowly dozed off and dreamed of baseball, rifles, and a red-headed woman.

Chapter Nine

The Visit

I awoke just before noon with my back hurting again. I stood up and stretched, then strolled down the hallway to my grandfather's bedroom. Music played on the radio, and Grandpa was sitting in the chair beside his bed.

"Hello," I greeted him.

Grandpa, wearing the nasal cannula, turned to face me. "Was your nap as uncomfortable as it looked?" he asked, grinning impishly.

"It beat my night in your sinkhole," I replied with a smirk. We laughed. I sat on the end of his bed. Bouncing up and down, I said, "This feels a lot better."

"Oh, no, no!" bellowed Grandpa. "There will be no trading beds. I'm not dying in a sinkhole."

Recalling the end of Grandpa's story about Mack, I remarked, "A sinkhole wouldn't be a 'glorious place' in which to die."

Always aware, Grandpa squinted his eyes at me. "You read about the rifle, correct?"

I nodded.

"And?"

"And then I went to sleep to restore my sanity!" I laughed, then added, "Those first two stories were torture. I hope I live through the next six."

"Me too," replied Grandpa, raising his eyebrows, and I caught the intentional double entendre.

"Uncle Mack was a great guy, wasn't he?" I said.

Grandpa sighed. "He was terrific. I always wanted to be just like him."

"Seems to me you're doing a pretty good job of it," I declared.

Suddenly breathless, Grandpa sat back in his chair. He gasped and coughed as I watched him closely.

"You OK?"

"Yeah, just dyin' is all," he answered. "Nothin' a sandwich couldn't cure."

I rolled my eyes. "Well, you'd better eat and gain some strength, 'cause you've got company coming this afternoon."

Grandpa glanced my way. "Who's that?"

"Robin Patterson."

Grandpa sat up taller and grinned. "How 'bout that sandwich then!"

I stood up, heading for the kitchen, but the gifts beneath our Christmas tree caught my eye. "By the way," I said, walking to the tree and picking up the baseball, "according to your story, this baseball is already mine. You've been keeping it for me, right?"

Grandpa chuckled, cognizant of my point. "Mister Smarty-pants!"

I laughed and set the ball down. "Does that mean I get the ball plus one other choice?"

Undaunted, Grandpa said with a wink, "You decide."

I left the bedroom smiling broadly at my grandfather's evasiveness.

The knock on the front door came at 2:45 P.M.

"I'm early!" announced Robin as we came face-to-face. She flashed a megawatt smile.

"Come in!" I said eagerly, holding the door. As she swept past me, the scent of her perfume filled the air.

"My grandpa's in his bedroom. I'll see if he's ready for you."

"Come on in!" he yelled down the hallway, so I led Robin to him.

"Hello, George. How are you?" she greeted Grandpa, who was sitting up in bed. He had set the nasal cannula aside for her visit.

"One foot in the grave and the other on a banana peel," Grandpa wisecracked.

Robin gave him a hug, then sat down in the chair. I sat on the end of his bed.

"How was church this morning?" he inquired, giving Robin his undivided attention.

"Good. Pastor Crandell prayed for you from the pulpit."

"Well, I hope he asked God for a Whopper and chocolate shake from Burger King," Grandpa declared half-seriously.

"That would've been a whopper if he had," kidded Robin, and we all laughed.

Playing the role of polite host, I asked Robin, "Would you like something to drink?"

She turned her ocean-blue eyes on me and shook her head. "Nothing, thanks. I'm OK."

OK? I thought. *That word doesn't cut it, not for the most beautiful woman in the state of Montana.* Or even in the world, as far as I was concerned. To keep my clammy hands from shaking, I clasped them on my lap, telling myself to keep cool.

Looking past me, Robin noticed the decorated blue spruce. "That's a pretty tree," she said.

"I put the star on top!" piped Grandpa, cheering for himself.

"How did you manage that?" asked Robin.

Grandpa chuckled mischievously. "I get by with a little help from my friends."

Robin laughed. "It looks to me as though you've got a few good friends, all right." She pointed a finger at the collection of objects beneath the tree. "Do I see a bunch of real money over there, or did you forget to put your Monopoly game back in the box?"

I grinned, admiring Robin's wit. "It's real money, but don't tell anybody. If word got out, a lot more of Grandpa's friends would start visiting, looking for a little help themselves," I answered for Grandpa.

Robin gave me a puzzled look, and I realized my comment sounded like an indictment.

Hauling my foot out of my mouth, I shifted the subject. "Uh, all those things under the tree are special to Grandpa." I glanced at my grandfather, hoping he would elaborate, but he kept silent.

With Robin and Grandpa both staring at me and the

moment growing more awkward by the second, I chose to keep talking. "You see, I get to pick one of the things under the tree for my birthday present."

Robin cracked a smile, then stung me by saying, "You mean you get to help yourself." I just about died, and even though she giggled and said she was joking, my face flushed for the second time in her presence that day.

This time Grandpa jumped in to save me. "Alan's birthday is next Sunday, Christmas Eve. He'll be twenty."

"Oh," said Robin with a nod. "I'm twenty too."

"You're twenty-two?" I blurted, raising my eyebrows. The inflection in my voice revealed my disappointment.

"No," Robin chuckled, "I'm twenty also."

"Oh! You're twenty, *too!*" I wished I could quit playing the fool in front of this woman.

"Yes. I turned twenty last June. June 16."

I grinned, feeling relieved. "You're just a few months ahead of me," I declared, happy for the closeness.

"Six months," corrected Robin, extending the distance.

"Yeah. Six months." I looked at the floor.

"So, then," said Robin, keeping the conversation moving, "what are you going to choose?" Lifting my gaze to her face, I saw she was smiling expectantly.

"I'm not supposed to decide until my birthday, and after I've read the story behind each gift." I glanced at my grandfather, hoping I hadn't told too much. He smiled weakly.

"What stories?" asked Robin.

Again I looked to Grandpa.

He stiffened. "I wrote a short story about each of the gifts, that's all," he spoke nonchalantly. I wanted to say how great I thought the first two stories were, but I held my tongue for fear of violating Grandpa's wishes.

Robin pressed the point on her own. "How many stories are there?"

Grandpa didn't appear too happy. "Eight," he said.

I held my breath, knowing what was coming.

"May I read them?" Robin asked eagerly.

I cringed along with Grandpa.

"Oh, you don't want to do that," he muttered.

"I'd like to," she persisted.

Looking uncomfortable, Grandpa replied, "Well, we'll see. Alan's reading the stories now. We'll see what happens."

Robin finally let go. "OK. Let me know, George."

He nodded.

Turning to me, Robin asked, "So, Alan, you're in college?"

Now I could impress her, I thought. "Yes, at the University of Michigan." I pointed at the Michigan sweatshirt I was wearing.

"Oh," she said, "the Michigan Wolverines!"

"That's right."

"What's your major?"

"Baseball."

Robin laughed. "All right, what's your minor?"

"Snow-skiing."

"And they give scholarships for those pursuits in the Midwest?" She wrinkled her nose.

"For baseball," I said proudly. "I'm on my own with the skiing. How 'bout you?"

"I'm in elementary education." There was a sparkle in her eye. "I want to teach little children."

"That's great," I said with enthusiasm. "Actually, I'm thinking about going into elementary ed myself!"

"Really? That's interesting."

"Do you have any scholarships?" I asked.

Robin shrugged, then nodded her head. "I've got a few, but they cover only two-thirds of my costs. I still need a few thousand dollars each year. I'm trying to get through college debt-free."

I heard the phone ringing in the kitchen. "Excuse me," I said, standing up from the bed. "I'll be right back." I hurried down the hallway and picked up the receiver. My mother said hello.

"Hi, Mom. Everything's going great."

"Good. Your dad and I were thinking about you, so we thought we'd call."

"Hi, son." My dad had been waiting on an extension phone. "How's the old man treating you?"

I winced. "Um, he's not that old. Only sixty-four."

"Oh," came the reply. "I...I'm sorry. I guess you're right."

My mother jumped back into the conversation. "What have you been doing lately?"

"You mean since yesterday?" I responded with some sarcasm, then I chuckled.

My mother laughed. "I know, I know," she said. "I'm a worrywart."

"That's OK," I replied, feeling close to her. "Let's see. I don't think I told you before; I cut down a Christmas tree, and Grandpa and I decorated it."

"Grandpa?" my dad exclaimed.

"Yeah," I said, smiling into the receiver. "He helped some."

"We thought he was dying!" blurted my mom.

"He is, but he doesn't want to die lying down."

"Lying down?" questioned my dad. "You mean, he wants to go down fighting?"

"No, not really," I said, looking for the right words. "Uh, he wants to go down living." That sounded good to me. I added, "He wants to die well. He—"

"It sounds like…like you're hitting it off with the guy," my dad interrupted. That sounded bad to me.

"I'm glad I'm 'hitting it off' with him, Dad," I said defensively. "He's my grandfather."

Silence burned a hole in our conversation.

My mother finally broke the ice. "Well, Alan, what else have you been doing?"

There wasn't much else to report. "Just talking," I related. "And reading a little."

"Oh, what are you reading?"

I decided to share a partial answer. "Some of Grandpa's stuff. He wrote some things."

There was a long pause on the other end of the line. I waited for a response, but none was offered.

Just then Robin entered the kitchen with Grandpa trailing behind her. I figured Robin was leaving. I knew Grandpa was staying, so without a second thought I handed him the phone.

"It's my mom and dad," I told him, and his eyes widened in surprise. "Say hello." He stood frozen, staring at me with both of his hands strangling the receiver. I smiled at him, then motioned for Robin to walk with me toward the living room.

As we left Grandpa to his task, I glanced back and saw him raising the phone to his ear. He squeezed out a greeting, which freed me from the long-distance conversation to attend to a very local one.

"I'm really glad you came," I assured Robin. "My grandpa thinks a lot of you."

Robin smiled shyly. "He's a wonderful Christian man. I wish he were healthy."

"Me too."

"I pray for your grandfather every day," Robin said tenderly.

I gazed into her shining blue eyes, and my heart executed what felt like a back flip with a full twist inside my rib cage. The sensation caused momentary breath loss.

"Um," I muttered, drawing some air, "I really appreciate it. Thank you, Robin." Her name rolling off my tongue sounded beautiful to me.

"You're welcome," she said softly. "Well, I'd better go. I want to fix dinner for my parents before church tonight."

"Church tonight?" I asked because I had nothing else to say. Robin's big smile, however, told me I had said the right thing.

"Yes. Wanna go?"

I raised my eyebrows and grinned at her. "Me?"

"Yes, you."

Like a fool, I hesitated. Certainly I wanted to get close to this woman, but I figured I would act like a dumb duck out of water inside a church, embarrassing myself.

"Well?" Robin pursued. Her smile was beginning to fade.

"Well," I said, thinking evasively, "I'd better just stay here with Grandpa tonight. You know…"

Robin looked away. "I understand."

I opened the front door for her, and she walked down the porch steps. As I watched her, I told myself I was crazy to reject her invitation.

"By the way," she said over her shoulder, "I was an All-Valley shortstop my senior year in girls' softball!"

"Wow! So you know baseball!"

She smiled and waved good-bye.

Bravely, I called after her, "Can I call you?"

"My number's in the phone book, listed under Ray Patterson." Robin climbed gracefully into her car and started the engine. I stood in the doorway as she drove away.

"That's the girl I'm going to marry," I found myself whispering. Shocked by the sound of my own statement, I said louder, "Hold your horses, pal! You just turned her down!"

Shaking my head, I stepped inside the house and closed the door on the subject.

Chapter Ten

The Money

Grandpa sat at the dining room table with his head bowed. I waited to approach until he looked up.

"How'd the phone call go?" I asked, sitting down across the table from him.

He looked at me with smiling eyes. "Not bad, considering it's been a long time since we've communicated. I'm thankful for the breakthrough and for you handing me the phone."

I laughed. "You should've seen your face. Your eyes got as big as platters!"

Chuckling, Grandpa said, "You know I've got a bad heart. What were you trying to do? Kill me?"

I shook my head. "No way," I replied thoughtfully. "I guess I was trying to heal you."

Grandpa's smile vanished. "Heal me," he said quietly. His blue eyes rimmed with tears as he pondered the thought. "Thank you, Alan."

"We're in this together, Grandpa—pitching and catching."

"Bottom of the ninth, right?"

"I guess so, but it feels like the first to me."

Grandpa rubbed away a tear. "Yes, in some ways, it feels like the beginning."

"Well," I prodded, "was the phone call any kind of a beginning?"

"I'm sure it shocked them to hear my voice, but at least they didn't hang up. They managed some civility toward me." He paused to catch his breath. "Anyway, they asked about the weather, how I was feeling, and how we were getting along."

"What did you tell them?"

Grandpa chuckled. "The weather's fine, I'm fine, and we're fine."

"Now I know where I inherited my telephone etiquette!"

He started to laugh, but suddenly leaned forward, slapping a hand over his heart. All color drained from his face.

I jumped to my feet. "Are you all right?"

Grandpa waved me off. Not easily dismissed, I scurried around the table to his side.

"Help me back to my room," he muttered. "I need some oxygen."

I hoisted him up, then half-carried him to his bed. He was the weakest I had seen him. After a few minutes on the oxygen, however, he seemed OK.

"Should I call your doctor?" I asked, sitting in the chair at his bedside.

"No," he said firmly. He adjusted his pillow behind his neck. "Like I told your parents, I'm fine. And whatever you do, don't tell Nurse Opal about this."

"Why not?"

"Because she'll stick me and poke me with every ice-cold instrument she carries in her medical bag!" he growled before coughing a half-dozen times.

I became concerned about his hacking.

"Don't worry," he said hoarsely, "I'm all right." He fiddled with the nasal cannula. "Anyway, your father's flying here on the twenty-fourth to relieve you of your duty. Reluctantly, I think."

"Being with you is no duty," I declared. "In fact, I think I should stay for Christmas."

Grandpa smiled softly. "That's a nice thought." After a moment, he surprised me with his next comment. "So, you're kinda hooked on Robin, eh?"

Squirming, I said, "It's that easy to see?"

Grandpa gave me a knowing look. "Even if I couldn't see it, I could still hear it in your voice. Every time you talk to her, you give it away."

I felt embarrassed. "Can Robin hear it too?"

"Is a baseball round? Of course she hears it. She sees it too."

I shook my head and gazed at my feet. "I must come across like a fool in front of her," I grumbled, feeling sorry for myself.

"Maybe, but it looks as if she likes fools!" Grandpa said, chuckling.

I raised my head. "What do you mean?"

He gave a short whistle. "It's written all over her that she's interested in you!"

"It is?" I asked dumbly.

"Sure." He pulled his blanket to his neck and closed

his eyes. "Trust me, she likes you—so relax. Just remember one thing."

He waited, so I asked, "What?"

He left me hanging for a moment to magnify the importance of the point he would make. Then he said quietly, "Robin's serious about God. So if you're not, leave her alone. She'll drop you before you get to first base."

My grandfather's words suddenly grabbed me like a choke hold.

"I'm serious about God," I said. I peered at my grandfather's upturned face, anxious for his response. He remained motionless, eyes shut, seemingly lifeless. I wondered if he were suddenly asleep or dead.

Then his lips barely moved as he said, "We'll see...."

I sat back in my chair and watched my grandfather nod off, not knowing what to think.

Something warm and moist lubricated my face while it was yet dark outside, arousing me from a nice dream about baseball. For an instant I thought someone was smudging my face with a rosin bag. Grabbing for it, my hand found Buck's mouth instead.

"I'm gonna wrap that tongue around a fence post!" I howled, sitting up. I pushed the light button on my wristwatch and saw that it was five in the morning.

"Great," I muttered, throwing off my blanket. The expected ache in my back was present as I hobbled to the bathroom. I flicked on the light, half-opened my eyes, and washed the dog saliva off my face.

Making my way through the living room by the glow from the wood-burning stove, I opened the front door and allowed Buck to charge outside. A blast of arctic air slapped me into full alert, and I quickly closed the door.

Chilled, I crawled back into bed, but after five minutes I knew more sleep was hopeless. The thought of reading two more of my grandfather's stories preoccupied my mind. I wrapped my blanket around my shoulders and walked barefoot to the kitchen, turning on lights as I went.

After pouring myself a glass of orange juice, I sat down at the table with the blanket draped over my lap. I picked up the manila folder marked "Money." I opened it, excited yet apprehensive, knowing this could be the story that told too much.

My eyes focused on the date the manuscript was written, and then there was nothing to hold me back.

11/09/93

I remember the day I first met Joyce. It was December 24, 1951. We were separately attending a Christmas party at the Menominee Gun Club in Michigan's Upper Peninsula. She was nineteen and absolutely beautiful. She had a look that would stop traffic.

I was twenty years old, as gangling as an orangutan, and had no intention of pursuing the prettiest girl at the bash. Doing just fine as an observer at the punch bowl, I planned to see a few old high school buddies, get a few laughs, then spend the night and Christmas Day with my parents, whom I was visiting.

Everything changed when Wilbur Smalley slipped a five-dollar bill into my hand with the words, "You can keep the money, George, if you get that girl out on the dance floor." Of course he pointed at Joyce, who had sat down at a table with a couple of girlfriends.

"It's a deal," I said with a gulp, needing all the money I could lay my fingers on for my college education. I pressed the currency into my pants pocket, handed Wilbur my punch glass, and started across the room toward Joyce. The closer I got, the more lightheaded I became. I truly believed I would pass out before I reached her table.

With money and manhood on the line, I cleared my throat and anchored myself to the wooden floor next to Joyce's table. When she looked at me, I worked up a grin and uttered, "May I have this dance?"

At first her face was blank, and I almost died on the spot. Weak-legged but ready to bolt away just the same, I prepared for rejection.

"Sure," was her simple response, but the shock of it caused me momentary paralysis. As Joyce stood up from her chair, I remained frozen in place.

"Well?" she said, waiting for me to escort her. I was shaking as we walked onto the dance floor.

The song was a slow one. She held out her right hand. I took it in my left. I curled my arm around her back. We danced. Somehow, thank God, I kept off her toes.

Two songs later, I was falling in love. Then Wilbur Smalley tapped me on the shoulder and tried to cut in. To my delight, Joyce told him, "Not now." And she and I danced away the night.

Almost twenty-seven years later, on October 26, 1978, I awoke at six in the morning, rising for my

*daily four-mile run. I gazed at Joyce's face as she
slept, noting the hardly faded beauty that still caused
my heart to race after twenty-six years of marriage.
I resisted the urge to kiss her, not wanting to take the
chance of waking her, and I slipped out of the
bedroom to the den, where my jogging shoes and
sweat suit were kept.*

*As usual, the den was cool, since it was our
custom to seal off the room at night to save on our
heating bill. Without a second thought, I followed my
normal routine and flicked the switch to an electric
space heater to knock off the chill in the room while
I dressed and stretched my legs.*

*Ten minutes later I was jogging through the
darkened streets of Ann Arbor, feeling quite peppy in
the brisk autumn air. A smile creased my face as I
thought about how good it felt to be alive. It was my
mother's birthday, and I looked forward to seeing her
that night and giving her the new coat my wife had
purchased as a gift.*

*When I reached the two-mile mark and the turn-
around point of my run, the same black mutt in the
same backyard started barking, as always. I shook
my head and chuckled, wondering how the owner put
up with it every morning.*

*A few minutes later, I heard a distant siren ahead
of me. I went back to my pleasant thoughts, ignoring
the sound as it quickly faded. My mind was on Joyce
and the surprise we had planned for Momma. My
only son, Dale, and his wife were in on it too, and I
couldn't wait to pull it all off.*

I should've noticed the black smoke in the bright-

ening sky sooner, but my fantasizing or runner's high
had absorbed my attention.

I got a sick feeling in my stomach. I knew my grandmother had died in a fire when I was two years old, but
the details, as far as I was concerned, had been sketchy.
Now they were to come at me, full blast, off a sheet of
paper. I could barely brave the heat.

Sweating, I pulled the blanket off my legs and tossed
it over another chair. I took a swig of juice, a deep breath,
and found my place in the story. I began with the ominous
sentence that had twisted my gut.

I should've noticed the black smoke in the bright-
ening sky sooner, but my fantasizing or runner's high
had absorbed my attention. Suddenly aware, I be-
came mesmerized by the rising cloud ahead of me.

Somebody's morning is getting ruined, I thought.

Figuring the smoke was billowing from about a
mile away, I was moving directly toward the source.
Something was burning in the vicinity of my own
neighborhood.

Then I remembered the electric space heater. I
had left it on. Only yesterday Joyce had asked me to
take a look at it, but I had forgotten about it.

I hurried my pace as fear screamed inside my head.
Two smoke alarms. The one in the dining room is a good
one, I told myself. But the one in our bedroom needs a
new battery. I had planned to buy one last week.

More sirens ahead. I ran faster. Sweat poured into
my eyes. My heart pounded; I heard it beating
against my temples.

When I finally entered my street, I saw fire trucks and police cars parked a hundred yards ahead of me. Are they in front of my house? Panic consumed me as I broke into a crazed sprint. Straining, driving, gasping, heaving.

My house! Towering flames! Crackling, exploding wood! Intense heat!

"Is my wife out?" I screamed at a hustling firefighter.

"Nobody came out!" he shouted, running to his assignment.

My eyes searched the crowd of onlookers whom two police officers were pushing back. "Joyce!" I wailed in their direction.

A policeman looked my way. "Get away from the trucks!" he barked at me.

"It's my house!" I bellowed back, tossing up my hands.

"It's too late! Get away!"

I turned toward my burning house. It was completely engulfed in flames. The fire hoses were spewing great streams of water—to little or no avail. I bent over at the waist and almost heaved my guts, but I didn't. Staring at my feet for several seconds, I watched a multitude of sweat drops fall from my face to the ground.

When I stood upright again, I was dizzy. "Joyce!" I cried, staggering along the sidewalk and into the street. "Joyce!"

People just stared at me, and there was no answer.

I waited two years to tell Dale that it was my negligence that had caused his mother's death. He knew *a short circuit in the electric heater had started the fire, but I had hidden the fact that Joyce had warned me about it the day before. I had kept mum about my forgetting to replace the dead battery in the bedroom smoke alarm; that is, until the guilt of my cover-up became too much for me to bear.*

In revealing the whole truth to him, I fell apart and wept like a baby. Dale comforted me initially, but then resentment over my remissness and my years of silence chewed hard at him. He became more and more bitter, evident most at birthdays and holidays.

Finally, my son cut me off from his family. He just walked away, rarely making further contact. I continued to live near him for several more years, hoping he would experience a change of heart. But his heart stayed cold and hard toward me, and I understood that the fire had taken more than my wife. It had consumed my entire family. It had torched my life.

Sometimes, in my darkest moments, I sit and wish Joyce had let Wilbur Smalley cut in on the dance floor and I had gone home. Then she probably would've lived a long, whole life. And I wouldn't have had to think about the money the insurance company paid me for her death. It's blood money. Money I cannot bring myself to spend.

I squeezed the last page between my thumbs and forefingers, unable to put it down. Rereading the final three paragraphs, I didn't know what to do. The answers to my questions regarding my family's dysfunctions were finally disclosed, but whether I should cry, call my dad, pull out my hair, or trash the room was beyond me. I inadvertently accomplished the latter, angrily taking a swipe at a teardrop on the tabletop and in the process knocking my juice glass and a couple of manila folders to the wood floor with my follow-through. The glass broke into a thousand pieces.

In frustration I kicked a chair on my way to fetch some paper towels, which stung the big toe on my bare right foot. Then I snatched the juice-spattered folders off the floor, took them to the kitchen, and shook slivers of glass into the sink.

"What's wrong?" sounded from behind me. I peered over my shoulder at Grandpa. He looked sleepy and disheveled. I looked wild-eyed and distressed.

"Everything," I moaned, feeling run through.

Grandpa stared at the pages lying on the table and slowly nodded his head. Meekly, he said, "Now you know."

Chapter Eleven

The Silver Key

"Can you forgive me, Alan?" Grandpa took a couple of steps toward me. His feet were bare.

"Watch out for glass!" I tossed the manila folders onto the counter and walked gingerly on the outer edges of my feet to my grandfather.

Extending my arms toward him, I said softly, "I forgive you. It was an accident." He fell against my chest.

"I'm sorry," he sputtered four or five times between labored breaths.

"Calm down, Grandpa," I said, patting his back. "It's OK." I felt him go limp, and it was all I could do to keep him from sinking to the floor.

"I killed her. That's what I couldn't bear to tell you, Alan. I killed her."

"Stop it or you're gonna kill yourself right here!" I jerked him upright and muscled him toward his bedroom. He shuffled his feet while I dragged him down the hallway.

"I love you, Grandpa," I assured him while lowering him onto his bed. I could barely see in the darkened room as I released him and he fell flat across the sheets.

Feeling for the nasal cannula, I scooped it off the floor beside the bed. I maneuvered Grandpa's body around and fastened the tubing to his head. I then collapsed in the metal chair with a sigh.

"I killed her."

I stared at the shape of his head lying against his pillow. "The fire killed her," I insisted. "You didn't."

He came right back at me. "That's not how Dale sees it."

Sadly, that was the truth. Grandpa's son, my dad, had remained unsympathetic and unforgiving.

Putting my father's bitterness aside, I asked, "How does God see it?" When Grandpa didn't shoot right back at me this time, I knew I had asked a rather good question. I repeated it.

Then Grandpa owned up. "I know God never blamed me; I just blame myself. It's been hard."

"I can imagine," I said. After a moment, I added woefully, "I'm sorry the family made it even harder."

My grandfather didn't respond, but I could hear him breathing more comfortably. I felt as though a most dreaded time for Grandpa had just passed, and we had made it through together. Closing my eyes, I was thankful.

"I love you, Grandpa," I whispered.

Quiet filled the room. Then Grandpa said, "I love you too."

Peace filled my heart.

Ten minutes later I had left Grandpa to his sleep and held the kitchen phone in my hand. Having dialed my parents' home, I thought I might catch my dad before he left for the accounting firm where he had been employed for sixteen years.

"Hello?" he answered after the second ring.

"It's me, Dad. You're up, aren't you?" It was 7:40 A.M. in Michigan.

"Alan? Everything OK?"

I felt my body tremble. "Grandpa needs your forgiveness, Dad."

There was a pause; then he asked, "What do you mean?"

I swallowed hard. "The fire was an accident, and you know it. How can you push Grandpa away?"

He waited again, obviously taken aback. Finally, he responded indignantly, "He got to you, didn't he?"

I stayed calm. "The truth got to me, Dad."

"The truth? He didn't tell me the truth of my mother's death for two whole years, Alan!" I could hear his breathing become heavier.

"Well," I said, "you haven't told me the truth of her death for fifteen years, but I'm not dumping you out of my life because of it, Dad!"

"Now wait a minute!" he raised his voice. "I was trying to protect you from the pain!"

I hated to clash with my father, but for my family's sake, including his own, he needed to realize what he was doing. "Pain?" I said. "Do you know what pain you've caused me by keeping me from him? It's pain that's been hidden from me all these years, and now it's tearing me up, Dad! Don't you understand?" I bit my lip and waited.

He didn't answer. I thought I heard him choking up as I pressed the receiver harder against my ear.

Quietly, I said, "Grandpa needs your forgiveness,

Dad. He's dying, for goodness' sake." Still no reply. "It's not that hard," I resumed. "Just three little words: 'I forgive you.'"

"I can't say those words," my father murmured.

"Don't you love your own dad?"

"Well," he said, clearing his throat, "I don't know. Deep down, maybe."

His words were the breakthrough I needed. Confidently, I stated, "Then please, Dad, start with 'I love you' and work into 'I forgive you.' You need to do it, Dad, for your own sake."

"I don't know."

"Pray about it," I suggested, surprising myself.

"Pray about it?"

"Yeah. Hang up and pray about it, then do what you know is right."

Once again my father was silent. I decided to close the communication on that note.

"Well, I'd better go. Give my love to Mom."

"OK," he said expressionlessly.

"Thanks for hearing me, Dad. I love you too."

"You sure about that?" he asked with a little more life in his voice.

I chuckled. "One hundred percent." With that, we hung up. I was shaking as I drew my hand away from the phone, but I was pleased with myself. Letting out a soft verbal cheer, I pumped my fist in the air like I sometimes did after fanning a good hitter. It felt good.

I remembered the wet manila folders I had pitched on the counter and the glass fragments and juice still on the dining room floor. Moving to the sink, I dabbed at the two folders marked "Baby Shoe" and "Santa Claus" with a paper towel and left them propped open on the counter to dry. Then I cleaned up the glass particles and juice puddles.

At a few minutes before six o'clock, I sat down at the table. I reflected on the morning's conversations with my grandpa and my dad, hoping for the best in each of their lives. Of course, Grandpa didn't have much time left.

I bowed my head and gave prayer my best shot. "God," I said, "I need your help." I hesitated, groping for the right words. Then, somehow, I sensed that I was trying too hard, that eloquence was unnecessary. All I had to do was say it.

"My grandpa needs my dad's forgiveness, and my dad needs to give it." There. I had hit the nail on the head.

I opened my eyes and stared at the tabletop. My prayer wasn't the greatest, but a prayer it was. My heart had been in it, and I knew that had to count for something. I looked at my watch, wondering what I should do so early in the morning. Naturally, my eyes fell next on the stack of manila folders.

"Something lighter would be nice," I said, shuffling through the pile. Two stories were wet on the kitchen counter, leaving six on the table, three of which I had already read. From my three new choices, I decided to try my luck with "Silver Key."

I opened the folder and lifted the typed pages from within. Setting them before me, I began reading.

1/19/92

At ten o'clock on the evening of September 22, 1973, Agnes Fritz called me on the telephone.

"It's time," she told me. "The sows are farrowing."

I hung up the phone and dashed out of my rental

house in Bay Port, Michigan, located a few miles inland from Saginaw Bay in the "thumb" of the state. Joyce and I had moved to Bay Port just over a year earlier, after Dale had gone off to college, as we were to spend three years of my teaching career in the area.

I ran to my blue Chevy pickup and started to open the truck door, but my eyes focused on my 1972 Yamaha YZ80 parked near at hand.

"I'll take my new bike," I decided. "The moon's bright enough to see the road." The motorcycle, which was an off-road dirt bike, was not equipped with lights.

I started up my bright yellow Yamaha and rode down South Bay Port Road, using the light of the moon to see. I hadn't bothered to put on a jacket. The day had been warm enough, but I felt chilled now as the wind bit into my face. My thin sweatshirt didn't lend me much warmth in the rushing evening air.

After three-quarters of a mile of problem-free navigation, I arrived at the Fritz farm. I shut off the motorbike and walked into the farrowing house. Forty-four-year-old John Fritz, my friend of a year, and his fourteen-year-old son, Jimmy, were inside the building ministering to three laboring sows. I joined them for the next hour and a half as we helped the sows give birth to twenty-five little piglets.

"Thanks for your help, George," John said to me when we were finished. "You're a good neighbor."

I left the farrowing house a shade after midnight. Climbing onto my motorcycle, I rode down the Fritz driveway to the paved road. The half-

moon illuminated the road as I shifted through the gears, accelerating until the bike was traveling fifty miles per hour.

A moment later, a cloud passed over the moon, hiding the moon completely. It was as though someone had flicked off a light switch, leaving me in total darkness. I stared ahead, looking for the big light another neighbor usually turned on by the edge of the road where some semitrailers were parked. I thought I could use the light as a guide.

Sure enough, I spied a light and aimed toward it; it was the wrong light. Seconds later, the motorbike left the road and went airborne. I found out later that the bike traveled seventy-five feet through the air, clearing a culvert, then smashing into a two-by-two-foot chunk of cement in a drainage ditch. I bounced off the bike and flopped for another thirty feet, ending up on my back in a washed-out culvert. My head, pounding with the pain of a concussion, was lying in two inches of water. My left leg lay across my right leg, grotesquely twisted and broken. My left pelvic bone was chipped. The ball in my left hip was shattered. Both ankles had fractures. My right arm lay across my stomach and made a crunching sound when I tried to move it; my right collarbone was broken.

"Gosh!" I exclaimed, shocked by the list of injuries my grandfather had sustained. I remembered hearing something about this accident when I was a child, but I had known none of the details.

Spellbound by the true story, I forged ahead.

As the motorcycle lay nearby with its motor still running, I tried to focus my eyes on my surroundings to see where I was. With a strange sort of timing, the cloud uncovered the moon, giving me the light I needed. I stared just in front of myself at the huge breakwall that kept the road above me from eroding into the hollow where I lay. I recognized my position as being in the fifteen-foot-deep drainage ditch off the edge of the road; it was the deepest ditch in the area. The breakwall was fifteen feet high and impossible for me to climb in my broken condition.

The water lapping at the back of my head was cold and annoying, so I needed to move. I tried to lift my left leg off my right, but the pressure was enormous. The leg would not budge. I used my left arm to shift my body until my head was out of the water. The pain that came with the effort was intense, and I was forced to rest with my head in mud and a moss pad wet against my back.

A minute later the motorcycle stopped running. I listened for sounds of life nearby and got excited by the sound of an approaching vehicle. I saw the reflection of headlights high above me in the darkness as the vehicle passed. I yelled, "Help!" with all my strength, but the vehicle continued on its way. I realized the night air was cold and guessed the vehicle's windows were rolled up tight.

After the third car had gone by with no one heeding my screams, I knew I was in a terrible situation. No one could hear my calls for help, my wife was far away visiting friends in Minnesota, and the air temperature was dropping into the thirties. I was soaked, and the thought of freezing to death crept into my mind.

I decided to steel myself and make an attempt at moving up the bank behind me. The bank was not as steep as the breakwall, yet it was just as high. Still not able to budge my left leg, I dug both elbows into the mud and shoved. The pain was so great I passed out.

When I awoke, the sun was shining on my face. It was eight o'clock in the morning. Unbelievably, I had been lying in the ditch for eight hours.

My face broke into a smile at the sight of the sun. I thought about how I must look—broken in pieces, wet and dirty, with a smile on my face—and I felt foolish.

To ready myself for the next vehicle, I dug both hands into the ground and pushed myself a foot higher on the bank behind me. My right shoulder literally snapped and crackled. I felt my consciousness slipping away in the knifing pain.

"Help me," I mumbled, and I stayed awake. I settled back on the bank and listened to a bird chirping in the distance. Looking in that direction, I saw the front wheel of my motorbike lying twenty-five feet away beneath some willow sprouts.

Then I heard a motor. As a truck came directly overhead, I saw its green roof. With all my might, I yelled, "Help! Help!"

The truck kept going. My heart sank.

Then I heard the truck's brakes and saw the green roof coming back. "Help!" I cried again. I heard the truck door open. A few seconds later, John Fritz appeared at the top of the breakwall.

"I'm down here! My leg and shoulder's broken."

John's mouth dropped open. "I'll go call an ambulance!" He ran to his truck, jumped in, and sped away.

A few minutes passed before Agnes Fritz drove up in another truck. She stood at the top of the break-wall and tossed down two blankets. They landed on my feet. I reached out with my left hand and pulled them to my chin.

Agnes spotted twenty-one-year-old Bob Ackerman feeding some cattle three hundred yards away on the opposite side of the ditch. She yelled and waved, beckoning him.

Bob ran across a plowed field and made his way down the embankment. He tucked the blankets around my body, sat down in the mud, and hugged me. A tingling of warmth ran through my body as he pressed his face against my cheek. His morning growth of beard pricked my skin.

"You need a shave, Bob," I told him.

"So do you," he said with a chuckle.

Soon John Fritz came back in his truck. Then I heard the welcome sound of an ambulance's siren.

There were a few more paragraphs to read, but I stopped for a minute and shook my head. I couldn't believe all that my grandfather had gone through. Each story, vividly revealing parts of Grandpa's life that had profoundly affected and shaped him, knocked me for a loop. I was keenly aware of the great privilege I was being granted, by him permitting me to read his personal stories.

Sighing, I looked at the last page of his writing.

I ended up having two operations on my hip, the latest of which occurred in May of 1975. A steel plate and four screws were removed during the second operation. Miraculously, I was left with only a slight limp for about six months, after which time I regained excellent health.

My Yamaha YZ80 suffered some extensive damage, but nothing my friend John Fritz couldn't fix. He took the motorbike home and repaired it as good as new. I let his son Jimmy ride it on many occasions until the end of the 1975 school year. Then Joyce and I moved to Ann Arbor, and I took the bike to use on backcountry bow hunts around the Waterloo State Recreation Area.

After moving to Montana in August of 1989, I used the bike on several early fall bow-hunting excursions. It was on one such trip that Keith Rowley, a local outfitter, led me to the Lord. To commemorate the event, Keith had a silver key made and a gold pendant inscribed with John 3:16, which was the Scripture verse he used to witness to me. The key fit my Yamaha YZ80.

The next time I used the motorcycle on a hunting trip with Keith, he said I was now "biking for Jesus." And that I was.

I smiled at the ending of the story. Slipping the pages back into the manila folder, I felt excitement growing inside of me. The motorbike had to be somewhere on the property, I hoped. Since the only place I hadn't explored was Grandpa's garage, I knew where I'd look first. I stood up from the table, grabbed the blanket off the chair, and headed for my bedroom to change into my clothes for the day.

If the cycle's in the garage, I thought, *I know right where to find the silver key.*

Chapter Twelve

Talking with Grandpa

The morning was still black as I opened the garage door. Unable to see a thing, I felt for a light switch. Flicking it on, I found myself standing beside a blue Ford Bronco. I also laid eyes on the bright yellow Yamaha YZ80, standing upright under a shelf full of miscellaneous junk. Despite its age, the off-road dirt bike looked new, which said a lot about Grandpa's care of it.

Taking the bike by the handlebars, I wheeled it out of the garage and onto the cement apron. With the bike discovered, I knew I would have some fun with it, although at the moment the morning was too cold and dark. I was well aware that the bike had no lights, and the sun wouldn't be up for at least another half hour.

I went back into the house and found my grandfather sitting up in bed with his table lamp lit.

"I got the fire going," I informed him. "The front of the house should be warm and toasty in a few minutes."

Grandpa nodded his head and invited me to sit down.

"Boy, it's cold outside this morning," I stated, briskly rubbing my arms.

"What were you doing? Getting wood?"

I grinned. "I was hunting for a motorcycle."

Grandpa raised his eyebrows. "You read about the silver key?"

"Yes sir, and what a story it was. It's amazing you weren't killed."

"I was pretty stupid, riding at night with no headlight."

He gestured toward the Christmas tree. "Get the silver key for me, will you?"

I got up and walked to the tree. Dropping to my haunches, my eyes fell on the stack of hundred-dollar bills. "Blood money," I muttered to myself, recalling my grandfather's loathing description.

"Here it is," I declared, carrying the key to Grandpa's bedside. He took it, then asked for his reading glasses and his Bible. I got them from his table.

"You saw the inscription on the pendant?" he inquired as I walked around the bed to my chair.

"Yeah."

He set the key ring on the bed and put on his eyeglasses.

"John 3:16," he said, opening his Bible to the passage. "'For God so loved the world that he gave his one and only Son, that whoever believes in him shall not perish but have eternal life.'"

Grandpa closed the Bible and took off his glasses. He shut his eyes. "I'll never forget the day Keith Rowley shared that verse with me, Alan," he said, seemingly reliving the moment in his mind's eye.

I relaxed in my chair, presuming my grandpa would tell me about it.

"We were sitting on a couple of tree stumps at the top of Shook Mountain, taking a break from elk hunting. The view was spectacular." He paused and ran his tongue around the inside of his mouth. "It was a view that went on forever, if you know what I mean."

"Yeah, I've seen pictures like that," I interjected.

Grandpa smiled, keeping his eyes closed. "It was September 27, 1991, about seventy degrees, and beautiful. Keith had bugled in a nice five-point bull just an hour earlier, and I had shot too high with an arrow. Missed him clean. How I missed at twenty-five yards, I'll never know!" Grandpa opened his eyes, making sure I was there, then closed them again.

"Anyway, that's when Keith shared that verse with me, which was about the third or fourth 'shot' he had taken at me—only this time he didn't miss. The arrow went right to my heart." Grandpa paused, and I kept quiet, letting him savor the recollection.

He ended it by saying, "I believed the Scripture on that mountaintop on that beautiful September day. And now I'm heading for heaven." Then he opened his eyes.

"Amen," I said, and since Grandpa smiled immediately, I was glad I had said it.

"You know, Alan," he said encouragingly, "you can do what I did."

I gave him a puzzled look.

"You can believe too. Then I'll see you in heaven one day."

I bit my lip.

"Trust the Lord," Grandpa clarified. "You see, the gift

of eternal life is the greatest Christmas present of all. You just have to accept it!"

I nodded. "Yeah, I'll think about it, Grandpa."

"Don't delay too long," he responded, squinting his eyes. "Christmas is upon us, Alan, and there's no better time to get right with God." He lay his head back on his pillow.

I sat quietly and chewed on Grandpa's words.

A few minutes later, I fed Buck outside, where it was still dark. Then I fixed a ham and egg breakfast, which I enjoyed but Grandpa just picked at.

After I had cleared his bedroom of dirty dishes, I grabbed *The International Thesaurus of Quotations*, the book that I had perused two days before, and toted it to Grandpa's room.

"Whatcha got?" he asked.

"I've got some famous quotations I wanted to ask you about," I replied, sitting down. "You marked some stuff regarding life and death."

My grandfather nodded, looking very old. "You're uncovering a lot about me, aren't you?"

"Yes."

"I knew you would, and I'm glad you have. I just hope you won't be driven away from me by all your discoveries."

I shook my head. "No way. I've been drawn closer. Much closer."

He smiled and gave me permission to ask my questions. I decided to read him the quotations he had underlined with ink, then get his reaction.

"Well," he said when I had finished, "life and death have been on my mind a lot recently. Actually, the subjects have been on my mind a lot for many years."

He coughed and fooled with the cannula for a moment. "Anyway, I've come up with my philosophy of life and death, Alan, and it goes something like this: Life is brief, often bumpy and tragic; a tough test. Death often rushes at us too soon and without mercy, but we can surprise it at the end because of God's saving grace." He stared at me. "That's it."

I shut the book and gave it a toss onto the dresser. "So, you feel you're ready to die, then?"

Without hesitation, Grandpa replied, "Yes, I am."

"And you feel you're dying well?"

Grandpa's eyes narrowed. "Yes, and you've helped me. You've given me just enough love so I won't have to die with a lonely, broken heart."

His comment made me feel good. "Thanks," I said, smiling.

I looked at the silver key lying on the bed. "Hey, since I found the motorcycle, how 'bout if I take it for a spin later? I need to see if I should choose it for my present."

My grandfather picked up the key ring and tossed it to me. "Just be careful or you'll be leaving this earth before I do!"

I grinned and slipped the key ring into my pants pocket.

"I've got one more thing to talk about," I said. "It's a proposal, actually." I glanced toward the Christmas tree and the money beneath its boughs. "Where does Robin work?"

"She works at an office supply store called the Darby Depot. She plans to work until August to get enough money to finish college."

"Then she'll go back to school for the fall semester?"

"That's her plan," affirmed Grandpa. "She's got some

scholarships, as she told you, but she needs another six thousand dollars."

"What about her parents?"

"They've helped a little, but like most in this valley, they don't have much money."

"So she's pretty much on her own."

Grandpa shrugged his shoulders. "That's about it. Our church took a love offering to help her last year. I remember it was close to seven hundred dollars."

I sat forward in my chair. "That's what I'm proposing, Grandpa. Helping her." I met his gaze. He looked as though he knew what I was driving at.

"I don't want to overstep my bounds, Grandpa, but why don't we just give Robin some of the money under the tree? You don't want it, and now neither do I. I've got a full ride at Michigan, and my family's pretty well-off, besides."

Grandpa pursed his lips, then wrinkled his face into a grin. "I'll tell you what: Why don't you deliver six thousand dollars to the Darby Depot in one hour, which is when one pretty young lady checks in for work? Tell her the money is hers if she'll go back to school next month."

I stood up from my chair with a "Hurrah!" I walked to the tree and knelt before the stack of currency. I broke the stack of bills in half and counted out six thousand dollars.

"Would Grandma be happy about this?" I asked, moving to the foot of Grandpa's bed.

He looked down at his left hand, and my eyes followed. I saw the gold wedding band he was regarding. He brought his hand closer to his face, then touched the ring to his lips.

"Yes," he said softly, "and she would be proud of you, as I am."

I smiled at my remarkable grandfather, feeling the weight of the wonderful gift in my hands.

Chapter Thirteen

The Ride

I arrived at the Darby Depot and parked my car in front. As I entered the shop, I saw Robin standing at the counter. She was the only person in the store.

"I brought you something," I announced, placing a brown paper sack on the glass countertop. My heart was pounding.

"What is it?" Robin asked with a smile.

"It's a Christmas present from my grandpa, but there's a condition attached."

Robin placed her hands on her hips and eyed the crumpled bag. "And what is that?"

I picked up a dust rag from the counter, dropped it on the glass, picked it up, and dropped it again. "Well," I said, "you've got to use the gift right away."

She frowned at me.

"It's for your education."

"May I open it?"

"Only if you promise to use it right away."

"OK," she pledged, lifting the bag. I held my breath as she unrolled the folds and peeked inside.

"What's this?" she exclaimed, flabbergasted.

"It's just some of that Monopoly money we had lying around beneath our Christmas tree."

Robin stood frozen, unable to speak.

"There's six thousand dollars there. Grandpa said it's yours if you go back to school in January."

She sank backward a step.

Smiling, I suggested, "Why don't you give your boss your two-week notice today?"

Robin suddenly folded up the bag and set it on the counter. "I can't accept this!" she declared.

"Why not?"

"Because, it's not right for me to take it."

"Why not?"

"Well, because it's George's, and he was giving it to you."

"What do you mean?"

Robin brushed a strand of red hair away from her eyes. "This money was one of the presents you could choose, right?"

I crossed my arms on my chest. "Yeah, Robin, but I don't need it. I choose for you to have it."

She looked confused. "Why give it to me? You hardly know me!"

I chuckled. "That's the beauty of pure benevolence, I guess! Who would do such a nice thing in this day and age, right?" Smiling for all I was worth, I answered my own question, "My grandpa, that's who!"

"And you, apparently!" Robin gushed. "I can't believe this!"

"Well, believe it. Just take the money and go get your degree. Then start teaching those first graders like you've dreamed about."

"Kindergartners," she corrected with a smile.

"Kindergartners," I repeated, smiling back. Our eyes locked, and I became self-conscious.

Looking down, I pointed to a smudge mark on the glass counter. "You missed a spot."

"Oh, sure. You made that when you were tossing the dust rag around!" We both laughed, making me feel more comfortable.

"So, then," I said, "can I tell Grandpa you accepted the money and his condition?"

Robin placed her hands on my shoulders, stood on her tiptoes, and kissed my right cheek.

"Give that to your grandfather for me," she purred.

"OK," I squeaked. Then she kissed me on the cheek a second time.

"That one's for you."

I was so ecstatic that when I left Robin I drove two miles out of town before I remembered I had planned to stop at Mr. T's. Making a U-turn on the highway, I went back and purchased some food for Grandpa and me.

When I finally arrived back at Grandpa's house, I found him taking his medications at the kitchen sink.

"I'm back," I announced as I walked in with my bag of groceries. Grandpa had his head tilted back with a glass of water to his lips, attempting to swallow a pill.

"Got some grape juice." I opened the fridge and set the bottle inside. "Some cereal and bread too." I moved to the counter where I had left two of the stories to dry. Setting the grocery bag down, I gathered the story pages together.

Grandpa's head dropped toward the sink, and he began coughing.

"Are you OK?" I asked.

He gave a little wave, letting me know he was all right. I watched him until he got control; then I placed the stories in their respective folders and left them on the counter.

"I'm fine," Grandpa assured me. He wiped the water off his chin and grinned. "That last pill went down like a brick!"

"Really? I didn't notice."

Grandpa smirked. "Let me tell you, Alan, the worst part is yet to come. Nurse Opal called about fifteen minutes ago. She'll be here any time."

"So? She told me she'd be back on Monday." I glanced at the date on my watch. "Today's the eighteenth. Monday." I looked at my grandfather and flashed him a smile.

"Wise guy," he muttered, shuffling toward his bedroom. "She wasn't scheduled to be here until three o'clock, and I told you I don't like her poking around. Don't tell her anything about yesterday afternoon when I slumped over in the dining room."

"I won't this time," I promised, following him, "but if it happens again—"

"—you still won't say anything," Grandpa finished the sentence for me. He glared over his shoulder. "Remember, I want to die right here, not in some sterile, ugly green, alcohol-smelling hospital room!" He kicked off his slippers and fell back into bed. I had to laugh as he grouchily slapped the nasal cannula onto his face and yanked his blanket up to his chin.

"I see you're adamant about this," I commented.

"That I am." His stern face looked out of character.

I heard a knocking at the front door. Grandpa heard it too.

"There she is!" he exclaimed. "She always knocks loud like that!"

I started for the living room.

"Pray for me!" Grandpa shouted after me. I looked back at his distressed face and flashed a smile. He didn't smile back.

When I opened the door, Nurse Opal met me with a businesslike look and an eager dog, Buck. The dog rammed his way between my leg and the door frame and headed for his master's bedroom. Opal wasn't quite as pushy, but almost.

"I'm in a hurry," she stated, entering the house. "How's your grandfather?"

I shut the door and tagged after her. "He's, um, doing OK," I replied, crossing my fingers as I said it. I wasn't lying, but I felt guilty about withholding the details.

"Has he been taking all of his medications?" she quizzed.

"Yes, right on schedule."

"See, I told you you could handle it."

"Yes, ma'am," I concurred. We entered Grandpa's room, and I had to fight to keep from laughing. He was lying in bed with his mouth open, pretending sleep even though Buck was nuzzling at his blanket.

Nurse Opal would have none of it. "Wake up, George!" she bellowed, sliding the chair out of her way and chasing off the dog. "Come on, Opal's here." She jabbed a thumb into Grandpa's rib cage. He fought off the first poke, keeping up his sham, but Opal's second dig was lower and could not be ignored.

"What's going on?" Grandpa cried, flying upright.

Opal dropped her bag on the bed and shed her coat. "Time for a complete checkup. I've only got fifteen minutes, so open your shirt."

I knew it was time to disappear. "I think I'll try the motorbike now, Grandpa." I smiled weakly at him. He bit his lip and reluctantly undid his shirt.

Opal unzipped her medical bag and took out her stethoscope.

"Don't worry," she said, sounding kinder as I left the room, "I'll be gentle, George."

"That thing's not ice-cold, is it?" I heard my grandpa plead.

I went to my bedroom and grabbed my baseball cap and a pair of leather gloves. Buck followed me outside to the garage. I dug the silver key out of my pocket and stuck it into the bike's ignition switch.

"Here we go!" I said to the dog as I straddled the motorcycle, my breath visible in the chilly air. I turned the key and kicked down on the starter. The engine gasped and died.

"Come on," I coaxed, hoisting my body higher over the bike. With a hard plunge, I slammed the kick-starter down, working the gas flow with my hand. The sound of the engine running was music to my ears.

"All right!" I slipped the cycle into first gear and was off. I rode the bike between the garage and the house, then past the barn. Buck bounded playfully along at my side.

I shifted through the gears as I sped across the field. Past the blue spruce trees I flew, too fast for the uneven terrain, too cold for my face, but too thrilling for me to back off.

By the time I reached the wooden fence at the end of the property, I had built a big lead on Buck.

I dropped gears and steered the bike toward the steep hill that I had avoided on my first day's jog. I looked for the whitetail buck in the trees, but he wasn't around.

I maneuvered through the woods, twice having to muscle the cycle over fallen cottonwoods, and once I plowed a deep path through a half-frozen, mushy patch of ground where a spring was flowing.

When I reached the far side of the woods, I stopped and put the bike in neutral. I wanted to make a charge up the big hill, which was covered with tall brown grass and lots of stones. Buck came up beside me and stared wistfully at the top of the hill.

"Wanna go up there?" I asked, watching my breath. Buck wagged his tail.

"Let's go!" I cried, clicking into first gear. Buck moved with me as I jerked the bike into second gear and swiftly accelerated.

As I hit the base of the hill, I drove into third gear for a good start. The hill was so steep that it stole all my speed in the first ten yards, forcing me to downshift and fight to keep the bike upright.

Sliding on some rocks, I shot stones off the back end, lost my balance, and dumped the bike to my left side, falling with it to the rocky ground. I turned off the motor, slid from beneath the bike, and sat in the grass beside the cycle. Buck stood next to me, oblivious to my problems. When I didn't get up soon enough for him, he began climbing the hill alone.

"You go for it!" I shouted. The dog kept going, bound and determined, it seemed, to make me look bad.

After a minute, I got up and gave the motorbike a brief visual inspection. It looked fine.

Gazing up the hill, I saw Buck reach the top and run silhouetted against the backdrop of the grayish, bright winter sky. He bounded, danced, and spun—even barked twice for show. I shook my head and pushed the motorbike down the hill toward the woods and the house beyond.

Chapter Fourteen

The Necklace

What happened to you?" Nurse Opal probed as we met on the front porch. I had just parked the motorbike in the garage and was heading for my bedroom.

"What do you mean?" I asked with a dumb look plastered on my frozen face.

"You're bleeding," she said, grabbing my chin. She eyeballed my left ear, then released me with a grunt.

"It's just a scratch, but dab some alcohol on it." She walked down the steps and headed to her truck. "Your grandpa's not doing too great. Keep his medication going, and I'll see you tomorrow afternoon."

I walked into the house, tossed my gloves and cap into my room, and went to see Grandpa.

"Did she leave?" Grandpa rumbled the instant he saw me. He was sitting up in bed, clad in his pajamas, with his blanket drawn aside. The nasal cannula was lying on the floor.

"Yeah. You all right?"

"That woman doesn't have much of a bedside manner. She pokes and pushes me this way and that, then has the gall to tell me I'll probably end up in the hospital in a day or two! Not on your life!"

I grinned, hiding my concern over Opal's prognosis. Grandpa continued glaring until the need to cough overcame him. He looked for the nasal cannula, so I got it for him.

"It's nothing," Grandpa said, getting the oxygen tubing in place.

"I've heard that before," I stated matter-of-factly.

"You don't look so perfect yourself. What's with the bright red face?"

I plopped myself down in the chair. "I rode your motorbike, and it's freezing outside. I tried to climb that big hill but decided to forget it before I wrecked your bike. As it was, I tipped over, but nothing got hurt."

Grandpa's eyes gleamed. "Like grandfather, like grandson."

"Maybe I'll end up choosing the bike as my present," I said, pulling the key out of my pocket and pitching it at the Christmas tree. It landed next to the Santa Claus costume. "Then again, maybe I won't."

Grandpa drew his blanket up. "You know, Alan, I may not make it to Christmas. It's a week away."

I saw he was serious. "Come on, Grandpa. Just yesterday morning you said you'd decided to live."

"No, son," he said quietly, "I said I was going to live a little longer, that's all. And guess what? I have!" He cheered up, causing me to smile. Continuing his thought, he added, "I don't think I'd have lasted this long without you around."

"Well, I'm still here," I challenged him.

"Lucky for me."

"Lucky for both of us," I asserted.

"Anyway, Alan, the nurse is probably right when she says my time is short."

"She told you that?" I wasn't happy with this.

Grandpa smiled slightly. "Oh, in so many words, she did. The fact is, I can feel it inside. I may die while you're still here, Alan."

A weak feeling surged through my body. Cognizant that Grandpa was studying my reaction, I deflected his gaze by looking down and rubbing my eyes. *What should I say?* I wondered.

"At any rate," he said, "why don't you go ahead and finish the last four stories? Read a couple more today and the others tomorrow, if you want."

I was surprised. "Really?"

He nodded. "You've already read the stories I was worried about. The rest are easier to handle, so read them while I'm still here. I want you to get done before Nurse Opal brings in the troops."

I stared at him.

"Go ahead," he encouraged me. "The nurse wore me out, and I need some rest."

Catching his drift, I stood up to leave.

"One more thing. How did Robin receive the money? Was she happy?"

I smiled. "She told me to give you a kiss for her, but I think I'll pass for now!"

"Quite frankly, I don't blame you," Grandpa joked. Then he laid his head back against the pillow, so I left the room.

Going to my bathroom, I looked in the mirror and

found my cut to be minor league. I decided to wash my ear along with the rest of my body in the shower stall, thinking a hot shower would do me good.

I was right. After the shower I felt warm and energized. I got dressed, then walked in high spirits to the kitchen. Looking out the window, I saw Buck standing near the barn. He was breathing heavily. I filled the teakettle with water and got a bowlful of food out of the pantry.

"Back from your triumph!" I hailed the dog. Buck trotted my way as I descended the porch steps.

"Thanks for coming back with me from the hill," I said sarcastically. I gave Buck a pat between the ears, filled his dishes, and went back into the house.

I took the two dried-out manila folders to the dining table, sat down, and thumbed through the entire pile of my grandfather's stories.

"'The Necklace,'" I read one of the titles aloud. Opening the top leaf, I slid the pages onto the table.

3/7/93

The Big Sky. Made in Montana, of course. When the Spirit of God was hovering over the dark surface of the earth and said, "Let there be light," the Almighty must have been directly above Darby, Montana. There cannot be a bigger, bluer sky under heaven than that which drapes across the awesome mountain peaks at the southern end of the Bitterroot Valley, sixty-five miles south of Missoula. Rarely a day goes by when Ol' Mister Sun is not seen and clouds are not as sparse as Rocky Mountain sheep ticks on a hot woodburning stove. Even in winter, the sky is often pure azure, free of gray paste, and the sun is a friendly and faithful companion. I know, because I live in this dry, sun-drenched land the locals have dubbed "The Banana Belt." In fact, a Chiquita brand sticker signifying "quality" is stuck right on the town of Darby on my Forest Service map. Quality—as in beautiful mountains, beautiful weather, and beautiful big-game animals. All three "beautifuls" perfectly mix each September, which is the "Month of the Bow Hunter." That's when every mountain within thirty miles of Darby is a hunter's paradise.

Since September in the Bitterroot can't be beat anywhere in the world, I make sure I find myself on a mountaintop when elk bugling is at its peak, which is the twentieth of the month, give or take a week. That's the season when dreams either happily meet reality or remain skulking visions in the forests, depending on whether the big bull comes all the way in for a face-to-face, up close and personal.

Desirous of an intimate meeting with a big bull elk in mid-September, 1992, a hunter's edict took me to the top of Rocky Knob: "If a bow hunter hunts elk in September in the Bitterroot, he should go high in elevation and hunt a north slope." On the north slope of the Knob, amid the balsa and Douglas fir, I sang elk songs with my reed-type elk bugle. It's the bugle that a friend of mine drove over with his pickup truck the year before, cracking the plastic mouthpiece. And even though it now bellows like the three-octave howl of a lonesome beagle, it gets the job done.

Weird-sounding as my call was, a distant bull echoed it for half an hour before he tired of my queer challenge and dropped me cold turkey. I couldn't blame him for not wanting to fight, on a delightful seventy-degree evening, what he had to think was some malformed troublemaker.

The following afternoon I went back with reinforcement in the bulky form of my friend Rick Scheele, the bugle-buster. Rick's a year-round T-shirt type, strong as a mountain lion but gentle as a newborn lamb. Strangers don't mess with Rick; if they did, he might love 'em to death.

At a spot close to where I had had all the action, I bugled and received a quick response from below us in the timber. Rick and I scampered fifty yards downhill, and I bugled again. The reply was loud and immediate.

"Dig in!" Rick warned me. "He's on the hook!"

Rick set himself up in a lodgepole pine thicket while I hunkered down behind two fir trees ten yards to Rick's left. I sounded my bugle again. A few seconds later, the bull retaliated from less than forty yards. His battle cry was just as raspy and distorted as my injured bugle. I would've chuckled but for the knot in my throat.

The knot suddenly became a grapefruit when El Wapiti leaped a deadfall fir tree and screamed his defiance once more. No kidding, Superman himself would've fled. I would have, too, if I hadn't been afraid that Rick would squeal on me.

Except for sweat glands leaking like broken hydrants and a heart pounding double-time, my body froze. The big bull stood rock still, too, and stared right through my camouflage paint.

Water slowly filled my eyes, and before I blinked,

the monarch turned off to the side. For a moment, I beheld his massive six-point antlers, rising like twin towers, looking perfectly symmetrical. Then I drew back my nocked arrow. I aimed and let the arrow go, then watched it fly past the huge chest. The bull whirled and disappeared down the slope, crashing branches as he escaped with his hide. I had missed. Thankfully, gentle Rick didn't seem to mind. Instead, he was thrilled that we'd invaded the bull's living room and had enjoyed a heart-thumping dialogue with one of creation's most incredible creatures. We went home happy for the paradisiacal experience.

The next day we went back and repeated the performance. Encore! I bugled; he came. Same act, different ending. Those six-point antlers now adorn Rick's living room wall, because Rick didn't miss. He gave me the bull's two ivory teeth, along with six ivories from other bulls he had taken, as my reward for having bugled the big boy into shooting range.

I took the eight ivory teeth to a local jeweler who created an exquisite, double-chained, beaded necklace that included the ivories, turquoise stones, and a diamond. The purchase of the thing was a splurge; in fact, it was foolish since there was no woman in my life to whom I could give the necklace. In retrospect, I think I simply enjoyed pretending that Joyce was still alive. She once told me of a dream she had had about a stunning necklace given to her by a handsome prince. Both of us laughed when she told me I looked nothing like the nobleman of her fantasy.

In some wild but wonderful way, I believe my securing of the elk-ivory necklace was a dream-

*like, befuddled attempt to become the prince of my
wife's illusion.*
   Crazy, huh?

I straightened the typed pages in my hands. "Poor
Grandpa," I muttered, shaking my head. I placed the story
neatly into its folder.
   "He's not crazy," I whispered. "He's terrific."

Chapter Fifteen

The Marathon

It was close to 12:30 in the afternoon when I heard Grandpa's radio. I walked down the hallway toward his room. A voice was saying, "For Breakpoint, this is Chuck Colson in Washington."

"You're awake!" I greeted him.

"Yes," he replied, almost too softly to hear. He didn't bother raising his head to look at me from his prone position. I wondered if he had grown weaker.

"We got a really nice phone call about an hour ago from Robin's dad," I said cheerily.

"Gerald," Grandpa acknowledged, staring at the ceiling.

I parked myself in the chair beside his bed. "He couldn't thank you enough for helping Robin finish her education."

Grandpa cracked a faint smile, then closed his eyes. I watched him quietly as he drew oxygen from the nasal cannula. His skin looked gray and frighteningly corpse-like, which repulsed me. Then I hated myself for my frame of mind. I wondered whether I would wimp out in the face of someone dying, especially when the one dying was determined to do it well. Could I watch well? I questioned my nerve. Would I hang in there?

Grandpa opened his eyes, found the radio lying next to him, and shut it off. Eyeing me, he asked, "Did you read any more of my stories while I slept?"

"Yeah, I read about the necklace."

"Uh-huh." He scratched his nose. "Did you like it?"

I knew exactly how to answer. "I liked you," I said with a grin.

He smiled back. "It's nice to be liked."

No longer was I repelled by the unhealthy look of my grandpa; rather, I was captivated by the real man beneath the timeworn surface. I loved his heart and his soul.

Yes, I told myself, *I will hang in there for this man.*

"How 'bout an early devotional?" he suggested with a livelier sentiment.

"Sure. I'll get it." I scurried around the bed and grabbed the small book. Sitting back down, I turned to the day's reading for December 18 entitled "God's Love on a Plate." The brief story, which I read aloud, told of Edith Schaeffer and her feeding the occasional vagrant at her home. She would prepare a meal fit for a king, then serve it along with a booklet containing the Gospel of John. The devotional went on to explain how those vagrants experienced God's love through Edith, and it finished by imploring the reader to serve up God's love to someone also.

"Then there's a verse printed on the side," I told my grandfather. "'Do not forget to entertain strangers, for by so doing some people have entertained angels without know-ing it.'" I looked again at the last sentence of the story. "'Through your generosity you will be serving Christ—and perhaps, you may be serving an angel in disguise.'"

I closed the book and looked at Grandpa. "That sounds like you."

"What?"

"An angel in disguise. Are you an angel in disguise?"

Grandpa snickered. "If so, I must be the angel who got last pick of the costumes!"

He made me laugh. "You're an angel as far as I'm concerned. I'll bet Robin would agree."

"Maybe, but Nurse Opal would argue the point."

"I suppose," I concurred, laughing again.

My angel wanted to shower and shave, so I helped him to his bathroom. Unlike the first day, he really need-ed my assistance.

"Want me to help you bathe?" I asked as he gripped the bathroom sink for support.

"Naw," he muttered, "I'll handle it."

While he was taking care of business, I vacuumed his room and made his bed. Then as I waited for him, I looked again at the photographs hanging on the hallway wall. The two of my parents with my sister Linda and me caught my attention. Both pictures had been taken when I was about eight years old and my sister was one, about a year before my grandfather's alienation. Linda, I sadly realized, knew virtually nothing of Grandpa, nor he of her. *An irreparable consequence of our family's breach,* I thought, shaking my head.

I heard the bathroom door opening and turned to meet Grandpa. He took my arm, and as we moved toward his room, I asked about the photograph of the wedding couple hanging above all the others.

"Momma and Poppa," he said, giving the picture a fleeting glance. "Reino and Marja, married in 1929."

"What were they like?" I wriggled the two of us inside the bedroom door.

Grandpa, breathing erratically, chuckled. "Finns and proud of it!" He lowered himself onto his mattress.

Taking the nasal cannula, he said, "You know that blue-and-white flag I stuck in the Christmas tree?"

"Yeah," I acknowledged.

He took a breath of the oxygen. "Let me tell you what my father did."

I drew the chair to the bed and sat down.

"On December 6, 1967, it was the fiftieth anniversary of Finnish Independence Day. I was visiting my father in Crystal Falls, Michigan, where a lot of Finns live. Dad decided to have a celebration like they do in Helsinki, a silent march in the streets." Grandpa paused to wipe his lower lip. "Anyway, he had two dozen of those Finnish flags, and we drove downtown to the drugstore. Dad made some phone calls and drafted every Finn he could find into taking a flag and marching up and down the sidewalks, and let me tell you, Alan, it was great. We walked together in twos, like a graduation procession."

"Wow," I said, "that sounds neat."

"Yes, it was. Some people driving by parked their cars and joined us, and others came out of the stores, as well. I'd say there were sixty to seventy marchers."

I grinned. "Pretty good for a spontaneous parade."

"Yes sir, it was something special. A silent march. I'll never forget the rhythmic pounding of shoes and boots on the cement. It sounded like the beating of a heart. And there was my father—leading the way, looking so proud…." A smile appeared on Grandpa's face, then faded slowly away.

Softly, he said, "I always wanted a son who would think as fondly of me as I did of my father that day."

We were quiet for a minute. I watched my grandfather's chest rise and fall with his breathing, but otherwise he lay motionless. Then he reached for my hand. I tightened my fingers around his.

"Dear Lord," he whispered, "thank you for sending Alan to me. You've given me peace, Lord, and I look forward to seeing you soon."

We continued holding hands, and I lightly rubbed the wrinkled skin on the back of his hand with my thumb. His eyes were closed, so I just sat still and waited.

After a few minutes, I got up from my chair and left the room. It was almost 2:00 P.M. I felt like taking a drive in the car, but I knew I shouldn't leave my grandfather alone for any length of time.

I sat down at the dining room table and stared at the pile of stories. "Three to go," I said under my breath, deciding to read one more. Selecting "The Marathon," I opened the folder.

4/28/92

In June of 1981, I was depressed. My wife had died tragically more than two-and-a-half years before, but it felt like yesterday. My son had been giving me the cold shoulder for several months since finding out I'd been holding back on the truth of his mother's death. My self-esteem was shot. My weight was up, mostly because I hadn't jogged a step since the fire had destroyed my house, my wife, and much of my life.

In mid-June, the Detroit Free Press printed an article on "How to Train for a Marathon." I read the story with some interest, believing I needed something, some goal, some reason to keep living. Included in the article was a four-month training schedule. Proceeding almost in a dreamy fog, I taped the schedule to the wall in my study and decided to begin training.

The first step was the hardest. By taking it, I felt as though I were somehow betraying my wife as I reentered an activity that had always brought me joy: running. I felt as if I was attempting to bury the past and forget about my wife, the thought of which appalled and scared me. I didn't want to leave my wife behind; I just wanted to leave my grief and find something to hold on to.

I took the first step, distraught and excited at the same time. It was good and it was bad. It was familiar, yet difficult. In the first mile, my legs felt surprisingly fresh, but I was still tortured in my mind. After two miles, my heart and lungs cried for mercy while my brain flooded with delight over my accomplishment. I stopped running with two-and-a-quarter miles under my belt, and I cried.

Standing in the middle of a vacant high school football field, I bent over and watched my tears fall to the ground, remembering the day my wife died. When I stood upright, I looked at the partly cloudy sky and smiled. I was hoping Joyce had seen my run from heaven and could rejoice in seeing me spring back into life again. At that moment, I resolved to run a marathon and to do it in her memory. A marathon: 26.2 miles. The toughest test I could imagine for the toughest comeback of my life.

I ran 100 miles in the first month, all at a pace of eight to nine minutes per mile. I knew I was on a "crash course" and wouldn't be in shape to race a marathon; I just wanted to run one in under four hours. A nine-minute-per-mile pace would allow me to achieve my goal.

I set my sights on the Skylon International Marathon on October 17. The course started in Buffalo, New York, crossed the Peace Bridge into Canada, and followed the Niagara River to the finish line at Horseshoe Falls. The 1980 Olympic Trials Marathon was run on this course. I figured if the course was good enough for Olympians, it was certainly good enough for me, a fifty-year-old retread.

With Niagara Falls on my mind, I increased my weekly mileage. Running six days a week, I was accumulating distance and experience.

During week seven, I ran a 10,000-meter race in Cadillac, Michigan, in 51 minutes and 41 seconds. At the end of week eight, I ran a very hilly half-marathon in Jackson, Michigan, in 1 hour, 52 minutes, and 39 seconds.

I shook my head in disbelief. Personally, I had never run more than five miles at any one time in my life, and here was my grandpa—at age fifty—running 6.2- and 13.1-mile races. I got tired and thirsty just thinking about it.

I got up, walked to the kitchen sink, and drank a glass of water. Filling my glass a second time, I carried it back to the table, where I resumed my reading.

During the next five weeks I ran more than 200 miles. It was difficult to rack up the mileage in October because the winds really blew on several of the days.

Nevertheless, October 16 came along, and I drove my car to Buffalo. I got a motel room, then set out to drive the entire marathon course in the car. I wanted to get a look at what I was up against before the next morning.

The course was beautiful. It was scenic, winding along the Niagara River, and it was mostly flat, which was a welcome relief after having tackled the hills in the Jackson Half-Marathon. At the end of the course was Niagara Falls, and I spent an hour there admiring one of God's best works.

The morning of the race was upon me before I knew it. I had had a restless seven hours of sleep, and when my alarm went off, I was up and dressed in my running clothes in fifteen minutes. I drove to the starting area at Buffalo's Bidwell Station. In the forty-four-degree temperature, I stretched out and loosened my body with the 1,688 other marathoners.

At 9 a.m. the starter called all of the runners to the starting line. I found a spot in the middle of the pack. After some last-minute instructions, the gun was fired. We were off.

Tears came to my eyes as I ran the first three hundred yards. My dream run had begun and my emotions overwhelmed me.

The first three miles were strange to me. My nervousness made me tight, and my legs did not respond well. I ran wobbly, like a newborn colt testing his footing for the first time.

After three miles, though, I loosened up, and all of the necessary coordination and fluidity was there. I ran like a mature stag, proud and sure.

I hit every mile marker for nine straight miles right on schedule, which for me was maintaining a nine-minute-per-mile pace. At the halfway point, I still felt terrific. But it was a long way yet to the finish line.

I cruised right along for four more miles. Then, just past the 17-mile mark, my legs began to grow weary. No real problem, but for the first time I was tired.

At 20 miles my right groin muscle started to hurt. Then a mile later I began experiencing constant pain in my left knee. The pain in both areas grew worse with every mile.

When I saw the 25-mile marker, my mind told me that I had only 1.2 miles to go, but my body was begging to stop. I staggered into a walk for 50 yards, then forced myself to run again. A few hundred yards later, I fell into another walk. Someone shouted that I had but a half mile to go, and I started running again.

"No stopping until I cross the finish line," I ordered myself.

It seemed like an eternity, but I finally rounded a bend in the road and spied the finish. Adrenaline flowed, and from somewhere within I found new energy. I picked up speed. The crowd of people lining the finishing chutes applauded. As I strained over the line, I *looked at my time on the overhead digital clock. It read 3:57:27, a time that will live forever in my mind.*

I had done it! I had run a marathon! I stopped running a few feet beyond the finish line. Though my leg muscles tightened immediately so I could barely walk, I sensed a rush of heaven. I had struggled through the end of the race, much like struggling through the tough times in my life, but it was all worth it in the end. I had made it to the finish, and it was great to be there!

The only thing missing was my wife, but I wasn't totally sure she was missing. Just in case, I blew a kiss to the skies.

"For you, my dear," I said. "Just for you."

I walked past other marathoners who were being hugged and congratulated by their friends and families. I smiled at those who glanced my way and found myself wishing I had someone in the crowd waiting for me, ready to embrace me and share in my achievement. But all the faces belonged to strangers.

Suddenly, though, my eyes locked onto a man about my age who was wrapped in a space blanket and had finished the marathon ahead of me. He broke into a wide, toothy grin and extended his right hand toward me. Eagerly, I shook his hand.

"We did it, ol' boy!" he declared with a victor's laugh.

Feeling good, I affirmed, "Yes, we did!" Then I laughed, too, shaking his hand long and hard. It was a wonderful moment, and afterward I felt strengthened to face the rest of my life.

Once again, I found myself blinking away a tear at the end of one of Grandpa's stories. His achievement, his fortitude, his gallantry, his loneliness—all of it tugged at my heartstrings.

What an interesting life! I thought. *What a great man!* And yet his wife had been killed, his son had abandoned him, he barely knew his grandchildren, and now he was dying at the young age of sixty-four. What trials and tragedies he had endured! It wasn't fair! Talk about a rotten deal!

Then I remembered something: Grandpa believed in God. That was the ticket to heaven, he had said. Not a bad deal after all, I realized, if Grandpa were right.

Heaven. Maybe things really would end up being OK for him.

The toughest challenge for me, I concluded, would be preparing myself for Grandpa's departure. I simply wasn't ready to see him go.

Chapter Sixteen

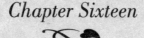

Pastor's Call

Buck met me at the back door as I stepped outside to enjoy a fellowship of sorts with the midafternoon sun. Even though the air was still cold, the sun's brilliance made the day nice.

I walked to the barn and called Buck inside, but like before, he wanted nothing of it and trotted away. I went to the big workbench where Grandpa's cardboard boxes sat. I disregarded those marked "Clothes" and "Books" and opened the others. Both boxes contained hundreds of black-and-white and color photographs of family and friends. There were also lots of knickknacks, a few outdated Montana hunting and fishing licenses, a collection of pocketknives, and a few other odds and ends. The most interesting item was a round bronze medallion inscribed with the words "American Institute for Public Service Jefferson Award, 1988, George Maki, in Recognition of Outstanding Public Service." The signatures of Jacqueline Kennedy

Onassis, Robert Taft Jr., and Samuel S. Beard were engraved on the medallion.

I wondered how such a prize ended up in the cardboard box rather than in Grandpa's safe. Deciding to amend this error, I slipped the medallion into my jacket pocket and left the barn.

I took a short jog around Grandpa's field just to get my heart pumping and feel the adrenaline rush. As I circled back, I saw a white car parked in the driveway and Buck dancing around on the porch beside a man in a brown trench coat.

"Hey!" I yelled, drawing the man's look.

"Hello!" he hailed with a wave as I approached. "I'm Pastor Tom Crandell. Is George all right? I knocked—"

"He was sleeping," I said breathlessly. Buck jumped off the porch, spun, and barked at the pastor.

"Quiet, Buck!" I commanded, climbing the steps. I introduced myself and shook the man's hand.

"Buck enjoys greeting me as vocally as possible," he chuckled.

I invited Pastor Crandell into the house and escorted him to Grandpa's room.

"Pastor!" my grandfather saluted his minister.

Keeping his coat on, Pastor Crandell sat in the chair at the side of the bed. "You're looking pretty chipper today, George," he said with a grin.

Yeah, Pastor, you should've seen him earlier! I thought. *He's putting on a good show right now.*

"I feel pretty good, Tom," Grandpa replied.

The pastor glanced at me. I wordlessly shook my head before Grandpa looked my way.

"I came to pray with you, George."

Grandpa smiled. "My biggest prayer has been answered, Tom." He nodded toward me.

I grinned, then excused myself to allow the pastor and Grandpa to speak privately. I used the time to look up Darby Depot in the phone book and dial the number. My heart beat faster as I waited for someone to answer at the opposite end of the line.

"Darby Depot, Robin speaking," came the voice I had hoped to hear.

"Hey, it's Alan. How are you?"

"How could I not be doing great after what happened this morning?"

"Did you tell your boss?"

"Yes, and he was fine with my going back to school. Whoops, a customer just walked in."

"When do I get to see you again?" I asked boldly.

"Well, how about if I drop by after work? Does that sound good?"

It sounded so good I almost dropped the phone from my sweaty hand. "Uh, yeah, that's great!" I uttered.

"OK, see you then."

"Oh, wait!" I blurted. "Will you do me a favor?"

"What's that?"

I quickly told her what it was; then we hung up.

I sat down at the dining room table and looked through the stack of manila folders, reading each title for the umpteenth time. I set the two labeled "Santa Claus" and "Baby Shoe" aside. They were the ones that had gotten wet and were now distinctly wrinkled. I decided to read them the next morning. Then I'd face my choice.

Which of the seven items left under the tree would I choose? I asked myself. I had ruled out the rest of the money, so what about the key to the motorbike, or perhaps the necklace? What about the rifle? Or maybe the baseball, although that was really mine already, wasn't it? Then there was the marathon certificate, plus I still didn't know anything about the bronzed baby shoe or the Santa costume. Which was the most valuable—not monetarily but sentimentally? What would I say to Grandpa about the reason for my choice?

I knew all the questions, but I didn't have any good answers. *Maybe I'll have the answers tomorrow,* I thought.

Pastor Crandell found me deep in thought at the table. I snapped out of it and got up to thank him for his visit.

"Your grandfather's a special man," he said warmly. "He's really happy to have you around."

As we walked through the living room, I said, "I'm glad I got the chance to come out here. Some good things have happened. I just wish they would've happened a long time ago."

"Better late than never," the pastor replied.

I opened the front door, and we stepped onto the porch.

"Alan, remember, George is going to be with Jesus. As a Christian, to be absent from the body is to be in the presence of the Lord."

I nodded. "Thanks, I'll remember that." I waved good-bye and went back into the house. Grandpa was staggering toward his bathroom door, so I helped him to the toilet, then waited in the hallway until he opened the door. He seemed completely worn out as I ushered him to his bed.

"You don't look so great," I told him, tucking his blanket around his body.

"I've been told that all my life," he joked.

I hooked him up to the oxygen, then sat down.

Grandpa noticed my stare. "What are you looking at?"

I decided to tell him exactly what I had been thinking. "I guess I'm looking at a man who's getting ready to spend some serious time with God."

He chuckled and drew in some air. "I can't go, though, until you make your choice, right? Did you read any more stories?"

"Yeah, the marathon one."

"And?"

"I can't believe you ran twenty-six miles."

"Twenty-six point two," he corrected me.

"Yeah, well, what I want to know is, what happened to your heart since then?"

My grandfather frowned. "That's a good question. I used to believe I had the strongest heart of anybody, but my family's history of heart disease finally caught up to me."

I leaned forward. "What do you mean?"

"Well," he answered, clearing his throat, "my father died of a heart attack at age sixty-two. When I was the same age, I was diagnosed with cardiomyopathy, which meant my heart muscle was deteriorating. It was becoming big and flabby, I guess."

"What about a heart transplant?"

"That was my hope, but my blood is thick. It clots too easily, and the doctor tells me I'm prone to strokes, prone to phlebitis, et cetera, et cetera."

"You should've tried another doctor and gotten a second opinion!" I said forcefully.

Grandpa smiled faintly at me. "The second opinion *and* the third opinion agreed with the first. Consequently, my name was placed way down on the transplant priority list."

Disgustedly, I sat back in my chair. "Well, then," I grumbled, "what about me? What about my heart?"

Grandpa's smile grew wider. "I love your heart, Alan."

"Aw, come on," I said with a shrug of my shoulders, "you know that's not what I mean! What about heart disease in my future?"

Closing his eyes, Grandpa sucked in a couple of breaths, then remarked quietly, "There's no heart disease in heaven, that's all I know for sure. There's no heart disease in heaven, thank the Lord."

Chapter Seventeen

Recitation

Robin knocked on the front door at 6:30 P.M. I opened the door and came face-to-face with a Burger King bag.

"Here's your favor!" Robin exclaimed.

I took the bag from her. "Fantastic!" I declared. We walked to the kitchen, where I mustered up a tray. Then I carried the food into Grandpa's bedroom.

"Surprise!" Robin and I announced together. My grandfather was sitting up, looking slightly healthier.

"What's this?" he wondered aloud.

"Yesterday you said you hoped God would deliver a Whopper and a chocolate shake," I reminded him. "Well, he came through!" Nodding toward Robin, I pluckily added, "As you can see, he sent the goods with one of his angels."

Robin smiled. "I think you two are the angels, considering the delivery this morning!"

I placed the tray on Grandpa's lap. He gave his hands

a clap at the sight of the meal. He immediately bowed his head and said, "Dear Lord, thank you for answered prayer, especially when it looks this good. Amen!"

Robin and I chuckled as he peeled the wrapper off the burger.

"So, Robin," my grandfather said, "you'll be going back to college and getting your degree, correct?"

"Yes, thanks to you," Robin replied with an affectionate grin.

Grandpa took a big bite. Suddenly remembering something, I excused myself and went to the dining room for my jacket. I delved into the pocket and found the bronze medallion.

Back in the bedroom, I held the treasure up for Grandpa and Robin to admire. "What was this doing in the barn?"

"You found it!" Grandpa exclaimed between bites. "It's supposed to go with the Santa Claus suit, but I forgot where I put it."

I wiped a smear off the face of the medallion, then had Robin read the inscription and signatures.

"That's wonderful," she said, visibly impressed.

Grandpa sucked on the milkshake straw, letting the twinkling in his eyes do the talking.

I took the medallion to the Christmas tree and laid it on top of the Santa costume.

"How'd you get it?" Robin inquired.

Grandpa smacked his lips. "Boy, I love the taste of chocolate," he mused. Then, gazing at Robin, he replied, "The governor of Michigan gave that to me in 1988 for my volunteer work with children. It was special."

"I'll bet," she said.

Grandpa bit into his burger, then said, "Anyway,

Robin, what are you going to do after you land a teaching position? Any plans for marriage?"

I almost choked on a french fry.

Robin glanced at me. I could tell she was embarrassed, but she bravely looked back at my grandfather. "Well, the right guy has to come along first."

Grandpa turned his eyes in my direction, which rattled me.

"Uh, you know, Grandpa," I blabbed, attempting to change the subject, "I was wondering why you moved to Montana. Why did you pick this particular place?"

Grandpa ignored my questions. "You know, Robin," he said quietly, "sometimes the right guy is already there, but you're just not paying close enough attention. Know what I mean?"

Again, I was dying inside. Scrambling to save the day, I squeaked, "Grandpa, did you hear what I said? Could you tell me what was so attractive to you about Montana?"

Robin, surprisingly cool in my estimation, turned toward me and smiled. I forced an awkward smile in return.

Grandpa took one more bite of his hamburger, then put the last portion of it on his tray. "That's about all I can handle. I don't have much of an appetite lately." He ground his teeth together, then took a drink of chocolate shake. "As to your question about moving to Montana, Alan," he said, swallowing, "I do have an answer for you."

I nodded my head encouragingly, happy to move our conversation along to another, hopefully safer, place.

"I wrote a piece about three years ago on the subject. In fact, I memorized it," Grandpa reported, handing his tray to Robin. She gave it to me as Grandpa began quoting his own writing.

"In the mountains of Montana, I find myself traversing in a dream world," he recited, resting his head on his pillow. "A world where mere humanity meets divinity. Where creation remains in its pure state, and sin and corruption find no one to seduce.

"I taste extrication and reprieve upon the mountain canvasses where God is the Master Artist. No ugly graffito stares at me from every brick wall because there are no brick walls. No vandalism on anything just 'because it's there' to ruin. Vandals don't climb mountains with paints and brushes. I guess that's because there are no traffic signs to deface. And that's a good thing, because I can't imagine a 'Yield—Right of Way' sign making things any safer for two bighorn rams on a collision course during rut."

Grandpa shut his eyes and continued. "The only things 'there,' in the land where I live and hunt, are what the Lord put there. And what he put there are eagles, elk, deer, bear, moose, sheep, goats, and lions. Not to mention trees, shrubs, rocks, berries, streams, sun, and the Big Sky. And peace.

"There's a 'peace that passeth all understanding' in the wild. There's beauty, and there's silence. I've seen sights that nothing man-made can match, and I've heard silence roar in my ears like Niagara. And when that silence finally breaks, it's not because of noise from a TV or a blaring radio. Instead, pure Mother Nature turns herself on in one form or another. Perhaps with heavy snowflakes tapping against the trees. Or with steady rain splashing off the brim of a hat. Maybe with the snort of a buck. Or with honking geese flying overhead. But the best audiovisual in the world is seeing and hearing an enraged bull elk bugle at thirty yards. If you've never experienced that, you've missed out on one of the surefire ways of fully discovering whether you're a man or a mouse."

Grandpa paused, and I found myself leaning closer to his bed than when he had begun his recitation. I glanced at Robin, perched on the edge of her chair, fully attentive.

"Let's see," Grandpa mumbled, endeavoring to pick up his narration. He scratched his forehead, then said, "When people ask me why I live and hunt in the mountains of Montana, I tell them 'for my own peace of mind.' You see, every time I climb the neighboring peaks, I meet myself. The clothes I wear don't mean diddly to the lodgepole pines. How much or how little money I have doesn't concern the deer. The bears don't care whether I'm short or tall, or whether I'm this color or that. A man's whole facade gets dropped up there in the hills, and the real, naked person stands up."

He stopped and looked sideways at Robin and me. "That's it," he announced, grinning sheepishly. "Does that answer your question, Alan?"

Fascinated, Robin said, "That was beautiful! I didn't know you could write so well!"

"Huh!" I said. "You don't know the half of it."

"That was great," Robin praised Grandpa again.

He winked at me. "Thank you both. And thanks for the meal. I've been dreaming about it for weeks! Now maybe I'll dream about something a little more daring, like jalapeno peppers!"

All of us laughed, and it felt good. There was no sense of death closing in on anyone, not at this moment. No feeling of loss, but only of gain. After all, we were having fun. Death seemed far away from my grandfather's little white house in Montana, where true love reigned.

Chapter Eighteen

Santa Claus

After a few more minutes with Grandpa, Robin and I left him alone in his room, concerned about tiring him. We ended up talking for two more hours in the living room. By the time Robin went home around 9 P.M., I knew she was meant for me. I didn't know how or when we would end up spending the rest of our lives together, but I knew I would work toward that goal. The next step, I decided, would be to tell Robin I really liked her. I guessed she knew it already, but I planned to look for the right moment to tell her before I flew back to Michigan.

After feeding the fire in the stove, I washed a few dishes, then looked in on Grandpa and made sure he took his medicine. I let Buck into Grandpa's room for a few minutes, then took the dog with me into my bedroom and crashed.

At 6:00 the next morning, I wandered to the dining room table in my pajamas. I had two stories to read, and there was no better time than the present, as my dad always said.

Since my curiosity had risen about the medallion, I chose the story titled "Santa Claus" over the other, "Baby Shoe." I spread the pages out on the table and began reading.

3/30/92

Dressed in a Santa Claus costume, I arrived at Menominee County Lloyd Hospital five minutes before I was scheduled to appear. I parked my car and darted to a rear door with a key the hospital director had given me.

Unlocking the door, I entered a tiny, dark room. The walls were stacked high with cases of pop and juices used to fill the hospital vending machines. Across the room, another door was dimly silhouetted by light seeping in around its edges. The door led to the adjacent hospital cafeteria, which had been gaily decorated and rearranged to accommodate the Christmas party.

The party was in progress. I heard the children's laughter and squeals, the old men's deep voices, and the nurses leading the program. Then I heard a youngster's raspy voice shout, "Where's Santa Claus?"

I threw open the door to the crowded room. "Here I am!" I laughed with glee as I entered to a roomful of cheers. "Ho, ho, ho! Hello, everyone!"

Two little girls raced up to me, and I squeezed them to my chest. "Merry Christmas!" I cried.

General chaos broke out. Children who were able to walk danced around me, punching at my big, soft

*belly and pulling my pant legs. I frolicked noisily
around the room, shaking hands with bedridden boys
and girls and old folks alike. I kissed an old woman
in a wheelchair, and she giggled like a five-year-old.
I got behind her and wheeled her around the huge,
decorated tree in the middle of the floor, laughing and
shouting and carrying on like a five-year-old myself.*

I threw my head back, picturing the hospital scene in
my mind. My grandfather playing Santa Claus was a
sight I would have enjoyed witnessing, especially as he
went wheelchair racing. The thought made me chuckle.

I turned my attention back to the story.

*Next I bounded over to a frail-looking girl who
had been solemnly watching my every move from a
bed that had been rolled in for the occasion. She was
snugly covered with a blanket. I lifted the blanket to
expose her feet and tickled them until she giggled.*

*"What do you want from good old Santa for
Christmas?" I asked her, lightly pinching her big toe.*

"A baby doll," she answered.

*"I'll see what I can do!" I laughed as I whirled
in circles like a spinning top. I spun over to an old
man who also was propped up in a bed. The man had
a small, gray beard, and I gave it a tug.*

"And what would you like for Christmas?"

*The old man grinned. "To be able to dance
around like you!"*

*I belly-laughed, leaned over the man's middle,
and scooped him out of bed.*

"Holy smokes!" he cried as I skipped around the

*room with him cradled in my arms. Both of us cackled
and cheered along with everyone else at the party.*

*The man's thin blue lips were wide with glee as
we weaved in and out of the other patients.*

*"Your Christmas wish has come true!" I said as
I put him back on his bed.*

*The old-timer's eyes danced with excitement, and
he announced breathlessly, "That was an awful good
present, Santa!"*

*I put my mouth next to the old fellow's ear. "I hope
I'm as lively as you when I get to be your age."*

*The old man winked at me, and I bounced away
to the center of the room.*

My grandpa's wish for liveliness at a ripe old age got
to me, because I knew his desire was not to be granted. I
sank my face down into my hands and listened to my
breathing. The refrigerator compressor kicked on in the
kitchen. I looked up, making sure I was still alone, then
my eyes fell back on Grandpa's writing.

*"Ho, ho, ho! It's time to pass out all these
presents!" I shouted. I sat down in a chair beside the
tree, and the children swarmed around me. After a
few hectic moments, the nurses managed to have
everyone sitting on the floor. Orderlies wheeled
bedridden and chairbound children to the periphery
of the semicircle.*

*As I handed out gift after gift, I studied the faces
of the children. Most were filled with vitality and
were relaxed, knowing that their stay in the hospital
would be short and basically harmless. For many of*

them, I thought, the visit here was a welcome change and, at this moment, much fun.

I looked at the faces of those children lying in beds. While their cheeks were tinged with pink from the excitement of the evening, the natural glow of youth seemed absent. Some faces looked sad even though the lips were upturned in smiles. That's the price of pain. The thought flashed through my mind in red neon lights. I wished there was something more I could do for those children besides simply playing Santa Claus.

When calling the names of those in the beds, I got up to deliver the packages. One frail little girl calmly accepted her gift and motioned for me to bend down close to her face.

"I love you, Santa," she whispered.

I looked into her pretty green eyes. One of them, her left, had a speck of harvest gold in it.

"I love you too," I said softly.

She smiled.

I gave her a kiss on the forehead. "Just remember," I cheered her, "Santa Claus loves you, so you get better!" With that I went back to the center of the group. I took a nurse by the arm and pulled her close to me.

"Is that little girl going to be OK?"

"Why, yes!" she assured me. "She has pneumonia, but she's getting much better."

"Merry Christmas," I told her, returning to my seat.

Later, after all the gifts had been passed out, everyone opened them simultaneously. The sound of paper tearing and excited squeals filled the room.

Santa Claus was no longer the center of attention, so I took that opportunity to leave.

"Merry Christmas!" I sang at the top of my lungs, making my way to the storage room door. I ducked into the room and out the rear exit.

Once inside the car, I took off my red cap and white beard and draped my arms over the steering wheel.

"Whew," I sighed. I was physically and emotionally exhausted. After a minute of rest, I started the engine and headed for home.

There was a gap on the page at this point. I paused to rub my eyes before sitting forward to absorb the remainder of the poignant story.

In March 1988, I was notified that I had been nominated by several people in my community for the distinguished Jefferson Award, which was news to me. In fact, I was one of ten winners in the state of Michigan. The awards, sponsored by none other than Jacqueline Kennedy Onassis, were given for outstanding public service benefiting local communities. I was informed that I was being recognized for my work with youth as a career teacher, coach, and (you guessed it!) Santa Claus.

Humbled by the ensuing media exposure, I joined the other recipients on April 7 at the State Capitol Building in Lansing, where the governor presented each of us with a beautiful bronze medallion. My English teaching staff, a few former students, and the hospital administrator from Menominee were my guests at the awards ceremony, making for a special day in my life. None of my family members were present, however, which was the only downside of the event for me.

As I retired to bed that evening, I realized that perhaps my life had accounted for something good after all, in spite of all the mistakes and tragedies I had faced. Perhaps I had benevolently touched a life here or there along the way, and maybe, just maybe, I would touch a few more in the time allotted to me.

I hoped so, · I remember thinking that night. I hoped so.

"Yes," I said, flicking my wrist and tossing the last page in the air above the table, "you did it, Grandpa!" The paper flew to the opposite side of the table, where it landed half on and half off. I jumped up and grabbed the paper before it fell to the floor, catching it just in time.

"Yes!" I proclaimed, jabbing the paper skyward above my head. "You did it, Grandpa! You touched my life! You touched me!"

In that moment, I felt like the most fortunate person on the face of the earth.

Chapter Nineteen

Attack

I took a shower and dressed before checking on my grandfather again. This time his light was on and he was hungry, so I went to the kitchen and made some oatmeal and toast.

I carried the breakfast on a tray into Grandpa's room and placed it on his lap. He said he wanted to give thanks to God, so I stood next to the bed and bowed my head.

Breathing rapidly, Grandpa prayed, "Dear heavenly Father, thank you for your love and care. We acknowledge you this morning as our Living Lord." He stopped and made a choking sound, causing me to look up. I watched him fidget with the nasal cannula, and his frustration was apparent.

Would he continue with his prayer? I wondered.

Sure enough, he said, "Thank you, Lord, for this sustenance. In Jesus' name, Amen." He opened his eyes and stared blankly at the food on his lap. His face was ashen-colored.

"Grandpa, are you all right?"

Nothing happened for a moment; then he lifted his gaze. His eyes looked hollow, but he grinned at me. Under the circumstances, I had to work to smile back.

Just as I turned away, thinking there was no immediate danger, Grandpa lurched forward and clutched at his chest. The juice glass spilled, but I grabbed the tray off Grandpa's lap and kept the bed dry.

"What's wrong?" I blurted, quickly setting the tray on the chair. He stiffened to an upright position, desperately trying to breathe. His eyes rolled back as he grasped his throat with both hands.

"Grandpa!" I cried. He looked at me with the wide, panicky eyes of a drowning man. Then saliva blew out of his mouth, followed by blood-tinged foam. He wildly jerked off the cannula.

"Oh, no!" I muttered. *What should I do?* resounded in my brain. "Hang on, Grandpa!" Down the hallway I ran, going for the phone. I ripped the receiver off the hook and dialed 9-1-1, praying the rural area had implemented the emergency service.

"Why didn't I check into this when I got here?" I scolded myself, hating my stupidity. Then the phone rang in my ear.

Someone picked up. "9-1-1 emergency," a woman's voice declared.

"I need help! My grandfather's having an attack!"

The woman told me to remain calm, then asked several pertinent questions before telling me an ambulance would come from Darby.

"Hurry!" I implored, hanging up. I raced back to the bedroom to find Grandpa rocking back and forth in his struggle to breathe. He saw me standing there, looking helpless, but his breaths were so stifled he couldn't speak.

The next seven or eight minutes were the longest of my life. I sat on the bed and held my grandpa as he gasped and frothed at the mouth. I assured him many times that the ambulance was on its way, but he offered nothing by way of acknowledgment. All his energy was focused on trying to breathe.

Once I jumped up and grabbed a napkin from the breakfast tray, using it to wipe the spittle off Grandpa's mouth and chin. He inadvertently knocked my hand away, though, as his body went rigid in the grip of a spasm. I was sure he would die any second.

"Please, God," I whined under my breath, "help us." Help came less than a minute later. I dashed outside as an ambulance roared up the driveway with lights flashing and siren blaring. Buck ran from behind the house and circled the ambulance when it stopped.

"He's in his bedroom!" I told the male driver as he climbed out.

A second EMT exited the passenger side and hurried to the rear of the ambulance, brushing Buck aside. "Down, Buck!" he said, evidencing a prior knowledge of the dog. He opened the doors and rolled out a portable stretcher, aided by a female attendant from inside. Then the female handed more equipment to her partners, some of which got stacked on the gurney.

"Let's move!" the driver said.

"Come on, Buck!" I called, hustling to the house. I grabbed the dog's collar as he bounded up the steps beside me; then I steered him into my bedroom and shut him in.

"This way!" I routed the EMTs through the house. We found Grandpa just the way I had left him.

The EMTs moved quickly. I stood clear as a stethoscope and blood pressure cuff were utilized. An IV was readied, Grandpa was hooked up to a heart monitor, and an oxygen mask was placed over his nose and mouth.

"Is he allergic to anything?" the female asked.

"Not that I know of," I responded.

Then the EMTs exchanged words like "D5W" and "blood pressure 162 over 98" and "He sounds real wet. I'm hearing rales and gurgles."

"Give Lasix IV push, eighty milligrams," directed one of the men, communicating on a walkie-talkie with a doctor in a hospital somewhere. "Monitor shows sinus tachycardia with multiple PVCs."

I looked at the heart monitor screen and saw an irregular rhythm.

"Morphine, four milligrams IV," barked the man with the walkie-talkie. The female EMT prepared a syringe. She no sooner jabbed the needle into the IV than Grandpa grabbed the oxygen mask and tore it off his face, panting for air.

"He's drowning in his own fluids!"

"Go get the portable suction!"

The second man rushed out of the bedroom. I moved farther from the action, ending up between the Christmas tree and the steel safe.

"He's got a lot of secretions, Mike," the female stressed.

Mike slipped the radio into a belt sheath and checked the monitor screen. "We'll intubate as soon as Cody gets back."

Twenty seconds later, Cody charged into the room with a portable suction unit. Telling my grandfather to relax, the two men worked an endotracheal tube down his throat. A catheter was inserted into the tube, then drawn out to suction the fluids from Grandpa's bronchial tubes. This was done several times.

"Everything's gonna be OK," Cody told my grandfather.

"He sounds clear now," Mike replied. The female EMT handed him the end of the corrugated plastic tubing that was attached to the oxygen tank. He joined it to the endotracheal tube, then wrapped a piece of adhesive tape around the point where the mouthpiece and oxygen tubing met. He secured the tape at the nape of Grandpa's neck to keep the endotracheal tube from slipping out of position.

After checking the heart monitor and Grandpa's pulse, Mike said, "We're ready to transport."

I watched the trio prepare to move Grandpa, then my gaze shifted to the gifts beneath the Christmas tree. I focused on the bronzed baby shoe, and it dawned on me that I had not yet read the story behind it. I wondered if my grandfather would still be alive when I read the story and made my choice. The choice would lose its meaning if Grandpa were dead, I told myself.

"Let's go," directed Mike, and Grandpa was hoisted onto the gurney. The female attendant covered Grandpa with a blanket while I scurried around the room gathering up my grandfather's slippers and bathrobe. Then I followed the procession out of the house, freeing Buck from my bedroom and grabbing my leather jacket along the way.

I yelled at Buck to stop him from pawing at the stretcher at the rear of the ambulance. Cody and Mike slid the gurney into the vehicle; then Cody and the female attendant climbed in beside my grandfather. I hurried to the front passenger seat, and Mike slid behind the steering wheel.

"You OK?" Mike asked, backing the ambulance around in the driveway.

"Yeah, I'm all right," I lied. I stashed Grandpa's slippers and robe on the floor beside me and looked at Grandpa's head just behind my seat.

"He can hear you, but he can't talk," Mike told me as we drove toward West Fork Road. "Obviously—he's got a tube in his windpipe."

"I'm right here, Grandpa," I said, and he looked up at me. His eyes showed confusion and fright, but he surprised me with a wink.

I heard Buck's bark and looked out the window to see him bounding alongside the ambulance. "Oh, no!" I groaned.

"Don't worry," Cody said. "He chased us down the driveway a couple of weeks ago, but he stopped at the road."

As Mike drove onto West Fork Road, I looked for Buck, but my view was obstructed.

Cody stared out a rear window. "He stopped at the fence line," he reported.

"Good," I said, looking at my grandfather. "After we get you taken care of, Grandpa, I'll get back here and take care of Buck. Don't worry."

Grandpa blinked his eyes once to show he understood. I reached over and lightly rubbed the top of his bald head. It was a loving gesture I would always be glad I had done.

Chapter Twenty

ICU

While Grandpa was in the emergency room at Marcus Daly Memorial Hospital in Hamilton, I found a pay phone and called my dad. I explained to him what had happened and told him to wait for me to call with further information.

Next I phoned Robin. She said she would get off work and come to the hospital but that it would take a while.

I sat down in an empty waiting room and leafed through a couple of magazines. Every ten minutes, I ended up back at the emergency room desk, hoping for an update.

Finally, after two hours, someone called my name. A white-coated doctor approached me. He looked young and wore a serious expression.

"Alan," he said, shaking my hand, "I'm Dr. Mayfield."

"How's my grandfather?"

"He's developed pulmonary edema. That's why he's short of breath."

"What do you mean?"

The doctor looked me square in the eye. "Your grandfather's heart is damaged. It's not pumping blood like it should. The blood accumulates in his lungs, so he has trouble breathing. That shortness of breath is called *dyspnea.*"

I nodded.

"Lasix has handled the problem so far, but as the heart gets further damaged, your grandfather goes into an acute condition. That's what happened today."

"So, what now?"

"We did a chest x-ray, EKG, and blood work in the ER. Now I'm trying to spiff him up in the ICU."

"Can I see him?"

"Yes, every four hours for fifteen minutes."

I couldn't hide my disappointment. "Dr. Mayfield, I'm the only relative he's got in Montana, and I'm only here for the next five days. Can't you—"

"I understand," he interrupted, smiling. "I'll instruct the nurses to let you in every two hours, but just go easy." He backed away. "If things progress well, he may be able to go home again." He gave me a nod and left.

When I entered the ICU, I saw my grandfather asleep in bed. The endotracheal tube was still in place. A corrugated plastic tube extended out to an in-line oxygen connection on the wall above Grandpa's head. He was hooked to a heart monitor and several IVs. There were sterile suction catheters and a suction machine next to the bed.

I sat in a padded vinyl chair and studied my grandpa's face. To my relief, his natural color had returned and his breathing seemed normal. He was definitely still numbered among the living.

"Grandpa?" He didn't move a muscle. "Grandpa?" I tried again, with no response. I sat back, leaving him to rest.

I closed my eyes, feeling fortunate I had made it through this crisis and that Grandpa was still alive. I asked God that if Grandpa were to die in the hospital there would be no more choking and foaming at the mouth, but that he would go peacefully.

Soon a nurse entered the room and suggested I go eat lunch in the cafeteria. She promised she would find me if my grandfather awoke. I took one more look at Grandpa, then headed for the pay phone.

I called my father again. I told him everything I knew, and we agreed he should hold tight and see how things developed throughout the day. Then I went to the cafeteria and bought a lunch.

A minute later, Robin approached my table.

"Hi!" I stood up and greeted her with a smile. I offered her a chair, then filled her in about Grandpa while I ate.

"A nurse is coming to get me when he wakes up."

"Will they allow me to see George too," Robin wondered, "or just family members?"

I grinned. "There aren't exactly gobs of family members coming out of the woodwork. You're as close as it gets."

Robin raised her eyebrows and smiled. "Just get me in, OK?"

"Just follow my lead."

Robin helped me polish off some potato chips, and as I finished my drink, the nurse from the ICU came over.

"Your grandfather's awake."

I stood up. "Let's go!" Robin and I followed the nurse out of the dining room.

The nurse looked at Robin over her shoulder. "May I ask who you are?"

Before Robin could respond, I blurted, "She's Robin Patterson, my fiancée." The nurse nodded once and turned away.

Robin's eyes bugged out. "Fiancée?" she mouthed the word at me.

"Almost," I whispered, shrugging. To my delight, Robin smiled, even though she was shaking her head.

The nurse led us to the ICU. I was thrilled to see Grandpa sitting up and looking at us with smiling eyes. With the endotracheal tube protruding from his mouth, he could only acknowledge us with a wave of his hand.

"Hello, Grandpa," I greeted him, and tears welled up in my eyes.

"Hello, George!" Robin said warmly. She bent down and kissed his forehead.

The nurse gave my grandpa a small pad of paper and a pencil. "You can use these to communicate," she said. Then she left us alone.

Grandpa laid the writing pad on his lap and painstakingly began to write. Since I hadn't brought his eyeglasses to the hospital, he squinted hard in order to see.

When he finished, he handed me the pad. The printing was scratchy, so I decided to pronounce each word out loud as it became clear to me.

"Alan," I read slowly, "I...almost...died. Next time...just...let me go." I glanced at Grandpa. He motioned for me to go on.

"My...Whopper days are...over...and I...want to go to...heaven. I love you...and...Robin too." As I said the last two words, I looked at Robin. Her eyes were misty.

"I love you too," she told my grandfather.

"You're the best thing that ever happened to me,

Grandpa," I said emphatically. Smile wrinkles tugged at the corners of his eyes.

Before the nurse came back, I told Grandpa of the phone calls to my dad and what Dr. Mayfield had told me. I believed Grandpa had the right to know what was happening inside his body, and he appreciated my telling him. Then the nurse asked us to leave.

I assured Grandpa I would round up some supplies for him and take care of Buck. "No fair dying before I get back," I ordered, jabbing a finger toward him as I moved away from his bed.

The nurse frowned, making it clear she didn't particularly like my gallows humor.

"You, either," I teased the nurse, popping a smile at her. She reluctantly grinned.

I took Robin by the arm.

"We'll be praying for you!" she assured Grandpa. Then we were gone.

Chapter Twenty-One

The Baby Shoe

During the trip from the hospital to my grandfather's house, I recounted the morning's frightening events for Robin as she drove us in her car.

"He doesn't have much more time, does he?" Robin uttered more as a statement of fact than a question.

"It doesn't seem like it," I said, gazing at the snow-capped mountains. "I just hope he recovers enough to get back home." I turned my eyes on Robin. "He wants to die at home."

"What about you? You're flying home Sunday, right?"

"I'm supposed to, but if Grandpa's still alive, I'm gonna stay."

"Sunday's your birthday, right?"

I nodded.

"Well, what do you want for your birthday?"

I laid my head back against the seat and sighed. "Well,

let's see. First of all, I don't want Grandpa to die on my birthday. How's that for a wish?"

"Understandable. I'll pray about that."

"Thank you," I said. "Secondly, I want to be able to stay in touch with you."

"Consider that present delivered."

"I was hoping you'd say that."

Robin pressed on the brake pedal and turned the car onto West Fork Road. "I'll give you my parents' address and a school address before you leave."

My heart leaped for joy.

A half mile later we turned onto my grandfather's driveway. Buck was lying on the front porch, and he jumped to his feet and ran at the car. Robin applied the brakes to avoid hitting the crazy dog.

"Buck!" I greeted him, opening my door. He licked at my outstretched hand.

"He likes you," Robin giggled.

I rolled my eyes at her. "Yeah, right," I said, downplaying the truth. "You wanna come in?"

"I'd better not—you know, with your grandfather not here."

I bobbed my head up and down. "Gotcha. Listen, thanks for the ride." I pointed at the rental car parked in front of us. "I can get back to the hospital just fine."

"OK, Alan," Robin said with a gorgeous smile. "I'll see you later."

"Bye," I said, climbing out. As Robin backed up the car, I shouted, "Thanks again for all your help!" She waved, and then Buck and I headed for the house.

I used the next hour to clean Grandpa's bedroom, wash dishes, stoke the fire, and freshen Buck's bowls. I found a sundry kit bag in Grandpa's bathroom already filled with bathroom supplies. I added his pill bottles to the bag. Grabbing his Bible, devotional book, portable radio, and eyeglasses off his end table, I carried the whole load to the rental car.

Remembering the manila folders on the dining room table, I went back into the house. My brain reverberated, *Take the last story with you.*

I scooped up the folder marked "Baby Shoe," then ushered Buck out the front door with me.

"You stay home, pal," I ordered the dog before starting the Ford Taurus. I drove to the end of the driveway and stopped while a pickup truck passed by on the main road. Buck used the moment to jump up and rub his wet nose across my door window.

"Down!" I hollered, giving the car some gas. I figured the dog would survive all right until I got home that evening.

When I reached the hospital, I grabbed Grandpa's gear and the manila folder and walked inside. The nurse at the ICU desk said I could visit for fifteen minutes.

"Hi, Grandpa," I greeted him. "I brought a bunch of stuff." I plopped everything onto the chair at the foot of the bed.

Grandpa nodded to show his approval, then pointed at the pencil and pad of paper on the table. I picked up the writing tools and gave them to him.

Grandpa scratched out a message. I silently deciphered the words, "Have you read all the stories yet?"

"No," I told him, "I've got one more, and I brought it with me."

Grandpa bobbed his head, then wrote another note.

"Let's talk turkey tonight," I read his message aloud.

I promised, "I'll read the story as soon as I leave here. It's about the bronzed baby shoe." Even with his mouth full of tubing, I could tell he was smiling.

I sat quietly with Grandpa for a while before he scribbled a final decree. It was to the point: "Get me out of here."

I hiked my eyebrows. "Anybody can see you're not going home today, Grandpa."

He shrugged his shoulders, implying that anything was possible.

I grabbed the manila folder from the chair. "I'll ask the nurse to take care of the stuff I brought," I said as I headed for the door. Then, waving the story in the air, I said, "I'll check this out right away. Get some rest."

Grandpa watched me all the way out the door.

I found the hospital's chapel. Since no one was there, I laid my jacket in one chair, then sat in another. I placed the folder on my lap and opened the flap. The story called "Baby Shoe" met my eyes.

12/24/92

One day I'll never forget as long as I live is Wednesday, December 24, 1975. On that day my grandson, Alan George Maki, was born.

I was enjoying the Christmas break from teaching high school English, relaxing at home with a good book, when the call came from my son, Dale. He told me Alan had been born just fifteen minutes earlier at 7:51 p.m.

"Your mother and I will be right over!" I told Dale. "Joyce!" I hailed after hanging up the phone. "We're grandparents!"

All the way to the hospital, I kept thinking, "I'm a grandpa. I can't believe it."

When I parked under a street light and got out of the car, my wife, as if she'd been reading my mind, exclaimed, "I'm a grandmother, George! I can't believe it!"

We entered the hospital and quickly found the nursery. Excitedly, we peered through the glass window, looking for our newborn grandson. Two babies were lying in their respective bassinets, but neither was named Alan.

A moment later, Dale came charging down the hallway. He gave each of us a bear hug and told us the baby was with its mother, Nancy. We joyfully followed our son down the corridor to our grandson.

After congratulating and planting kisses on Nancy, Joyce and I took turns holding Alan in our arms. The first thing I said to him was, "Welcome to the world, kid." Then I felt his right bicep and told Dale, "He's going to be a fine pitcher, just wait and see."

At ten months, Alan was taking big steps in his first pair of baby shoes. He was also entering a "throwing stage" in which toys were flying halfway across various rooms due to a good right-hand delivery. "I told you so," I remarked to Dale one day as we studied Alan's wobbly windup, toss, and follow-through. "We didn't have to wait too long, did we?"

When Alan was fifteen months old, Dale and Nancy presented Joyce and me with one of our grandson's first shoes after having it bronzed. I held the cherished shoe in my hands and unwittingly *began rubbing the side of it. Joyce stopped me when she asked if I were trying to get a genie to come out of the shoe.*

I responded by saying, "No, but a genius has already come out of it." Of course, I was referring to my grandson. I believed anyone who could figure out how to wind up and fire a fastball at ten months of age had to possess superior intelligence.

About three months later, when Alan was a year and a half, I was sitting in my son's house and Alan was playing on the floor beside my chair. Suddenly he began choking. His eyes grew large and he couldn't catch his breath.

I picked Alan up and pounded him on the back; that didn't work. I opened his mouth and saw no obstruction.

"Please, God, make him breathe!" I pleaded.

I don't even remember all that I did. I think I tried the Heimlich maneuver. At any rate, he finally started breathing. He sobbed between every breath, and I hugged him for a long while.

I realized then that I would die for my grandson. If there were ever a situation in which one of us had to go, I would step forward. I knew my love for Alan was that great.

As I sit alone in my house in Montana on this cold December 24, 1992, it is Alan's seventeenth birthday. I wish I could be there, celebrating with him and his family back in Michigan, but it's not going to happen. Maybe next year, or the one after that. I'd love to watch him blow out the candles and open his presents. I'd love to shake his hand and tell him what a man he's turning out to be.

It's dark outside, and I hold Alan's bronzed baby shoe in my hands. It's so tiny. Gently rubbing the side of it, I make a wish: Maybe next year, or the year after that.

I searched for another page, but there were no more pages. The story had ended, short and bittersweet. I closed the folder and stared out the window, momentarily paralyzed with the realization that, not only had the story abruptly stopped, but my reading of Grandpa's stories was finished. The reflections of his life were over. The revelations were closed, ceased, terminated. I now knew everything. There would be nothing more from Grandpa to hang on to.

I sat back in the chair, feeling as if a rug had been pulled out from beneath me. My grandfather was dying; his life was ending. I was scheduled to go home, to move on. It all seemed so unreal, so imaginary.

Chapter Twenty-Two

Pondering the Choice

Just before 5 P.M., I checked with the nurse at the ICU. She told me my grandfather had fallen asleep but I was welcome to sit in the room with him.

I tiptoed to the foot of Grandpa's bed. The chair was devoid of the things I had left there, and I sat down so softly I never made a squeak.

Grandpa was breathing well, giving me confidence he would awaken soon and hear me make my anticipated choice. There was only one problem: I didn't know what to choose. I had seen all eight of the items and read all eight of the stories, and now that I should have known what to pick, I knew nothing of the sort. What should I take? What would anyone take?

I closed my eyes and pondered all the angles. When I looked at Grandpa a couple of minutes later, he was staring at me.

"You're awake!" I stated the obvious. I got up and stood beside his bed.

He held up a previously prepared note.

"Have you...made...your choice?" I read aloud. I looked at Grandpa's eager eyes and my heart sank.

"Listen, Grandpa," I said, groping for words, "I've read all the stories....I love all the stories. Every gift is special. I just need a little more time. I want to do the right thing."

Grandpa picked up the pencil and paper from the bed. He wrote a new message while I brooded over my feelings of incompetence. When he finished, he handed me the whole pad.

I read, "You are wise, Alan. Pray...and...sleep on it. God will...give you the answer. Don't worry."

I bent down to rest my head on my grandfather's stomach. He put his fingers in my hair as I hugged him tight. We stayed like that for what felt like a long time, clinging to one another, and it was beautiful.

After speaking with both Robin and my dad on the phone that night, I went to bed. Buck curled up on the floor beside me, but he was restless. He got up every twenty or thirty minutes to check whether Grandpa was back in his bed.

By one in the morning, I'd had enough of Buck's commotions. I moved both of us into Grandpa's room to end Buck's pacing. I crawled into my grandfather's bed and was reminded how a real bed felt.

I thought I'd fall quickly to sleep now that Buck was quietly sprawled out on the floor. But as the dog snored, I tossed and turned, pondering the choices lying beneath the Christmas tree only a few feet away. *So close,* I thought, *and yet so far.*

Disregarding Buck's contentment, I flicked on the table lamp, then climbed out of bed and sat on the floor next to the tree. Buck looked at me but didn't bother to unfold from his comfort zone.

I fixed my eyes on the presents, wishing for one to jump out. When I finally determined that none of them was going to talk to me, I stumbled back into bed. Turning out the light, I recalled Grandpa's words: "God will give you the answer. Don't worry."

I lay my head on Grandpa's pillow and closed my eyes. In my own greenhorn way, I asked God to help me fall asleep. I focused on drawing deep breaths, relaxing each limb, and thinking about nothing.

Finally, I slipped over the edge of awareness, but only for a moment. I suddenly shot up, eyes wide open.

"I got it!" I shouted. Buck flew to his feet.

"It's OK, Buck," I said more calmly. I put out my hand, and he came to it. "Everything's all right," I said, petting his head. "Really all right!"

I fell back onto the pillow, corralling my emotions for the dog's sake. "We can sleep now, Bucky-boy, because I've made my choice." I pulled the blanket up to my shoulders, satisfied.

A minute later, Buck slumped to the floor, and we both drifted off to the land of Nod.

Chapter Twenty-Three

The Choice

An alarm rang incessantly in my ears, and when I groggily reached for my watch to turn it off, I realized it was the phone that was ringing. I scrambled out of bed and ran in the dark for the kitchen.

I knocked the receiver off the hook and onto the floor, but quickly scooped it up and blurted, "Hello?"

"This is Liz at Marcus Daly Memorial Hospital. Is this Alan Maki?"

My pulse quickened. "Yes."

"Dr. Mayfield wanted me to call you right away, Alan. Your grandfather has taken a turn for the worse, and you should come to the hospital."

I flicked on the kitchen light and saw that it was five in the morning. "What's going on?" I insisted.

"Come to the ICU desk. Dr. Mayfield will speak to you, OK?"

My hand began trembling. "OK," I consented. Then the line went dead.

Half an hour later, tousled but wide-awake, I stood face-to-face with Dr. Mayfield.

"Your grandfather is getting weaker," he told me. "The oxygen saturation in his blood is not as good as it was."

"What's that mean?"

"His heart's not pumping effectively, and his breathing's more labored."

"Is he gonna die?"

The doctor gave me a firm look. "If there are any other people who need to be here, you'd better call them."

I understood. "Can I see my grandpa?"

Dr. Mayfield smiled softly. "Sure. He's awake on and off."

"Doctor, he wants to die at home," I reminded him.

"I know, Alan, but I'm afraid that's not going to happen."

I went to the pay phone and called my dad in Michigan. I begged him to catch the next plane to Missoula.

"It's your last chance to talk with him, Dad," I pleaded. "Can you get here today?"

My dad hesitated. "Boy, it'll be tough."

"Please, Dad—come."

I listened to my father's breathing. Finally, he said, "I'll try, Son."

I gave him a hospital telephone number and hung up. Then I went to see Grandpa. He was lying on his back, looking sickly. He shakily handed me a piece of paper.

I discovered it was one from the day before. "Have you made your choice?" it read.

Touching his hand, I posed a question of my own. "I can choose any of the gifts that were in the safe, right?"

Grandpa nodded.

"OK, Grandpa," I announced boldly, "I know what I want." I swallowed, then stated, "I'll take…the stories."

He gave me a startled look.

"I want the eight stories," I repeated. I could feel my face glowing.

Grandpa fumbled for the writing tablet and pencil on the bed. I helped him, and he wrote one word: "Why?"

I rubbed my chin, wanting to choose my words carefully. I knew my reasoning was important to my grandfather. "Because with the stories, I get my grandpa back. I want my grandpa, and there's a big piece of you in every story." I paused, then added, "Life is in the stories, Grandpa. Your life. That makes them more valuable than anything else."

He closed his eyes, seemingly thinking over my words. Then he wrote another message.

"I'll bet you were smarter than Berryman," the note read.

I laughed. "You remember the name of the valedictorian!"

Grandpa's eyes twinkled.

I persisted, "Can I keep the stories?"

He slowly nodded his head, and I pumped a fist in the air.

"Thank you, Grandpa," I said tenderly. "I love you."

He held up his trembling hands for an embrace, and I fell into his arms.

Grandpa was asleep a few minutes later, so I sat in the chair, watching and listening to him breathe. It was a time of quiet, a time of repose. A time for me to feel our connectedness: young man to old man, grandson to grandfather, two generations apart yet closer than mere human blood could bring us. Only a greater power could have accomplished the miracle I had experienced over the past few days with this dying, princely man.

I closed my eyes, fighting back the tears.

Grandpa slept for several hours, and there were moments when I thought he'd never wake up. A couple of times he took what appeared to be his final breath; then as I moved to his side, he gasped and breathed again.

In the early afternoon, Dr. Mayfield had me leave the room while he examined my grandfather. I stood anxiously at the ICU desk until the doctor emerged.

"He's awake, Alan, but his heart's giving out. I don't think he's got much time left, so make it count." He smiled kindly and left me to my task.

Grandpa's eyes were open, but he waited until I took his limp hand in mine before looking at me. Even his stare was weak.

"I love you, Grandpa."

I thought he tried to smile, and then he let go of my hand and fingered the blanket alongside him. I knew he wanted the paper and pencil, so I got them for him.

Grandpa's hands were quivering, and he dropped the pencil twice, but his perseverance won out.

I took the paper and studied his scribbling. I saw there were two words, and after some difficulty, I realized what they said.

"Choose Jesus." I gazed into my grandfather's eyes. They were edged with tears.

Grandpa blinked, causing the tears to run down his cheeks. Then he shut his eyes. I waited for him to open them again, but he didn't.

I grasped his hand and bowed my head. "I choose Jesus," I prayed quietly. "I want Jesus in my life, because I believe."

I looked up at Grandpa. He kept his eyes closed but gently nodded his head. I knew he had heard me, and he approved.

I sat down in the chair and thought about the choice I had made of the eight stories and the choice I had just made concerning Jesus Christ. The more I contemplated the two choices, the more I decided that, for me, they were practically the same.

In choosing the stories, I had placed high value on my grandpa's life. In treasuring the stories, I had treasured all that my grandfather was about. I had rejected nothing he had written and nothing he had stood for. Everything had rung true in my heart. That being the case, in earnestly choosing the stories, I also affirmed Grandpa's God, at first without comprehending it.

"I choose the stories," I reiterated in a whisper, "and I choose Jesus with them."

By the time 2 P.M. rolled around, I had been sitting in Grandpa's room for more than eight hours. A nurse had come to see if Grandpa would eat anything, but he slept through her visit and the subsequent delivering of a meal for me.

After eating, I had a tough time staying awake. Grandpa's loud breathing had fallen into a steady rhythm that lulled me closer and closer to dreamland. I didn't want to fall asleep, just in case something happened, so I fought it hard. Eventually, though, my eyelids drooped shut, and I was out like a light.

Chapter Twenty-Four

Good-bye

Perhaps an hour later, I was aroused by something—a presence in the room. My body was sprawled in the chair, and as I cracked open my eyes, I sensed a figure standing to my right. The person's silhouette was backlighted by the outside window, and my eyes needed a moment to focus on the face.

Suddenly startled, I jumped up and exclaimed, "Dad!"

"I made it," my father said as we hugged.

"I'm so glad you came," I told him, looking toward Grandpa and hoping he was awake. He wasn't.

"How's he doing?" my dad asked.

I shook my head. "He's weak, and his heart's bad. The doctor says he's near the end."

Dad moved to Grandpa's side and stared at his father's blanched face. "He's aged a lot since…" He caught himself and looked at me. Realizing I knew his thoughts, he went ahead and finished, "…since the last time I saw him, years ago."

I stepped next to my father. Draping an arm around his shoulders, I said soothingly, "I'm glad you're here, Dad."

He kissed my forehead and thanked me.

When my grandfather woke up for the last time, he found his estranged son kneeling at his bedside. Tears flooded his eyes when Dale held his hand and asked Grandpa to forgive him.

Then, as my father climbed onto the bed and embraced Grandpa, I heard him whisper, "I love you, Dad."

With my heart in my throat, I walked to the opposite side of the bed and lay down beside my grandfather. I wrapped my arm around both men and pulled us close.

A wonderful thought came to my mind, so I said it. "You're back home, Grandpa. You're home."

He put his cheek against mine, and the touch said it all. The three of us lay side by side for a long while. For most of the time, we just listened to each other breathe—in and out, together, unified. A rekindling. A rebirth. A resurrection of family. I clung to every moment.

When my father finally spoke, he spoke first of regrets and of pardon, and when that was finished, he spoke of good times. He spoke of great times. And he shared the love that had been simmering in his heart all along.

As Grandpa lay listening, a quiet peacefulness settled upon his face. Finally, he let out a sigh and closed his eyes. His body tensed slightly, then relaxed as he drew a full, final breath. In that moment, he died.

When the nurses and doctor came, I kissed Grandpa's cheek before moving away from his body. My dad took my arm, and we walked toward the door. My heart was pounding so hard I thought it would break through my chest.

At the door, every limb of my body went numb. Gasping for breath, I made myself turn back one last time to look at my grandpa. I had to wipe my eyes in order to see him.

"I really love you, Grandpa!" I declared with the little strength I had left. "You are the best!"

How do I walk away from my grandpa? I asked myself. *How do I walk away?*

You just do it! I scolded myself. *Just do it!*

I stared at Grandpa's body another second, freezing his image in my mind; then I did it. I turned and walked away.

Outside the ICU, I saw Robin hurrying down the corridor with a nurse. As she came to me, I saw tears in her eyes.

"He's gone," I told her.

"I know," she said, hugging me.

"This is my dad, Dale Maki," I managed.

Robin shook my father's hand and handled the rest of the introduction herself, saying, "I'm Robin Patterson, a friend of George and your son." She looked at me. "A good friend."

"Nice to meet you," my dad replied, smiling warmly.

"I've been in the chapel, praying," Robin informed us.

I started to speak, but she placed her fingers to my lips to hush me.

"It was your time to be with him," she said; then she looked toward my father. "Yours and your dad's."

I understood.

"Besides," she added, "I wanted to remember him the way I last saw him."

Me too, I thought, for I had last seen him with his life reconciled and resolved. At peace. And in the hands of his Lord.

My father and I dropped off his rental car and drove to Grandpa's house in mine. Dad met Buck in the usual manner—in the driveway with Buck all over him. Then I showed him Grandpa's place.

While Dad made a phone call to my mother, I went to Grandpa's room. Standing just inside the door, I stared at the gifts beneath the tree until my eyes, at last, focused on Grandpa's bed and the chair beside it. The bed and the chair, Grandpa and me. In my imagination, I could see the two of us talking back and forth, sharing remembrances of the decade that had passed us by.

Suddenly inspired, I walked to the tree, bent down and picked up the baseball. Rotating it in my hand, I was surprised to find fresh writing on it. In ink, it read, "Happy Birthday, Alan, my angel. Pitch a few good ones for me. Love, Grandpa."

I cradled the ball with both hands and cried.

Over the next three days, my dad and I did what needed to be done concerning Grandpa's estate. I also spent some quality time with Robin, and our relationship grew despite the sad circumstances.

I decided to let Robin read Grandpa's stories, and she read them all in one night. When she gave them back to me, emotion overcame her as she expressed how much the stories had meant to her. Once again, we hugged one another, this time for a long while.

On Sunday afternoon, which was Christmas Eve and

my twentieth birthday, Robin and I parted after promising each other we'd get together again soon.

"I'll be praying for you," were her last words.

"I'll be dreaming about you," I said, waving good-bye.

She flashed me the warmest smile in the world.

That same evening my dad and I took a plane home to Michigan with Buck and a bronze casket aboard. The casket was buried in a family plot next to a gravestone that read, "Joyce Ellen Maki, Beloved Wife and Mother."

Not many people attended the graveside service—just the family, a few friends, and a half-dozen of Grandpa's former students—but those who did attend were deeply moved. The estrangement had ended. New lives had begun—thanks to my special, unforgettable grandfather.

Love Inspired® SUSPENSE

RIVETING INSPIRATIONAL ROMANCE

Watch for our new series of
edge-of-your-seat suspense novels.
These contemporary tales
of intrigue and romance
feature Christian characters
facing challenges to their faith...
and their lives!

Steeple
Hill®

Visit:
www.SteepleHill.com

Love Inspired.
HISTORICAL
INSPIRATIONAL HISTORICAL ROMANCE

Engaging stories of romance,
adventure and faith,
these novels are set in
various historical periods
from biblical times
to World War II.

NOW AVAILABLE!

Steeple
Hill®

For exciting stories that reflect traditional values,
visit:
www.SteepleHill.com